el

Praise for

MY REAL NAME IS HANNA

"Masih maintains a perfect balance of pacing and tension, and in Hanna creates a strong and inspiring young female protagonist. Elegantly detailed. . . . Highly readable and affecting, it's a haunting and hopeful work that deserves a broad audience. And at this particularly divisive time when fear and intolerance are constantly crowding the headlines, this book offers seeds of compassion to young and experienced readers alike."

—*Small Press Book Review*

"Every now and again I read a book that affects me so profoundly that I have to take a day or two to process what I have read. This was one such book and it completely took my breath away."

—*Left on the Shelf Book Blog*

"Hanna's story brutally captures the slow, relentless creep of wartime chaos into ordinary lives, then uncovers an astonishing, rich vein of hope in a world gone utterly dark. The anguish and love painted here are both timeless and timely."

—Elizabeth Wein, *New York Times* bestselling author, *Code Name Verity*

"*My Real Name Is Hanna* is a stirring story of survival, resilience, and love. Masih breathes life into the smallest of details, and gives us a powerful look into a world not often explored."

—Crystal Chan, *Bird*, shortlisted for the Waterstones Children's Book Prize, winner of the 2015 Burr/Worzalla Award

Praise for

MY REAL NAME IS HANNA

"From the very first lines, this is a beautiful, compelling story. . . . In bringing light to the caves of memory, Tara Masih gives us the redeeming power of storytelling in this extraordinary story."
—Bobbie Ann Mason, PEN/Hemingway Award winner,
In Country

"*My Real Name Is Hanna* is an emotionally-charged tale of survival against all odds. It is both a sensitive coming-of-age story of a young girl in hiding from the Nazis, and a testament to the rare compassion of neighbors in an otherwise hostile environment."
—Sharon Hart-Green, *Come Back for Me*

"*My Real Name Is Hanna* is a beautifully told and deeply moving novel. Masih is to be commended for shining light on a little-known piece of Ukrainian history. . . . This novel is about the stories that surround and sustain us in the darkest times—from the histories in the trees and in the ground beneath us to the words that feed us."
—Tilar J. Mazzeo, *New York Times* bestselling author,
Irena's Children, a *New York Post* 2016 Best Book

MY
REAL
NAME
IS
HANNA

MY REAL NAME IS HANNA

Tara Lynn Masih

[M]

Mandel Vilar Press

This book is typeset in Dapifer. The paper used in this book meets the minimum requirements of ANSI/NISO Z39.48-1992 (R1997). ∞

Cover and text design by Sophie Appel

All part quotations are from *Personal Recollections of Joan of Arc*, by Mark Twain (1896)

This is a work of fiction. While some settings, events, and high profile figures are based on reality, the characters are drawn from the author's imagination. Any resemblance to actual persons, living or dead, is purely coincidental.

Publisher's Cataloging-In-Publication Data
Names: Masih, Tara Lynn
Title: My real name is Hanna : [a novel] / Tara Lynn Masih.
Description: Simsbury, Connecticut : Mandel Vilar Press, [2018] | Subtitle from cover. | Interest age level: 12 and up. | Summary: "A riveting story about how a Ukrainian Jewish teenager and her family attempted, with cleverness and courage, to escape the Nazis." —Provided by publisher.
Identifiers: ISBN 9781942134510 (paperback) | ISBN 9781942134497 (ebook)
Subjects: LCSH: Holocaust survivors—Ukraine—Juvenile fiction. | Jewish teenagers—Ukraine—Juvenile fiction. | Fathers and daughters— Juvenile fiction. | Immigrants—United States—History—20th century—Juvenile fiction. | Jewish historical fiction. | CYAC: Holocaust survivors—Ukraine—Fiction. | Jewish teenagers— Ukraine—Fiction. | Fathers and daughters—Fiction. | Immigrants— United States—History—20th century—Fiction. | LCGFT: Historical fiction.
Classification: LCC PZ7.1.M3754 My 2018 (print) | LCC PZ7.1.M3754 (ebook) | DDC [Fic]—dc23

Printed in the United States of America
18 19 20 21 22 23 24 25 26 / 9 8 7 6 5 4 3 2 1

Mandel Vilar Press
19 Oxford Court, Simsbury, Connecticut 06070
www.americasforconservation.org | www.mvpress.org

This book is dedicated to the Ukrainian Jews
who did not survive the Holocaust, and to those women
and men who did, such as the resilient Esther Stermer,
Zhanna Arshanskaya, and Wilhelm Dichter.

It is also dedicated to those Galicians, Ukrainians,
Poles, Russians, and peasants who risked their own lives
(and sometimes lost them) in attempts
to save their Jewish neighbors.

Long ago, people believed that spirits and ghosts lived
in the ruins and caves. Now we could see that there were
none here. The devils and evil spirits were
on the outside, not in the grotto.

ESTHER STERMER, *Holocaust survivor*

All sorrows can be borne if you put them
into a story or tell a story about them.

ISAK DINESEN, *author*

MY
REAL
NAME
IS
HANNA

The Story Begins

I WILL SAY MY real name to you for the first time. Hanna Slivka. Don't be scared. I am still your mother. Born on February twenty-second, in the winter of 1928. Your grandmother often told me to remember this date because that is the day that God allowed me into this world to breathe my first soul breath of chilled Ukrainian air. She remembered the smell of the air that morning, too, while lying in her birch bark bed. She said it smelled of pine pitch from the new slatted wood that Papa had planed and hammered together to expand their one-room house. They had to make it larger to provide room for me, their firstborn.

She told me all this as we sat in fear for our lives in the dark. That our people believe the breath of life—*neshamah*—is holy. That she could see snow falling outside the window, great big flakes like goose feathers. And a bantam cock crowed, she said, as if to welcome me.

My family told stories. We swallowed them in place of food and water. Stories kept us alive in our underground sanctuary. The world continued to carry out its crimes above us, while we fought just to remain whole below.

Yesterday, daughter, you found my copy of *Joan of Arc*, hidden under dark rafters for many years. Musty, foxed with brown spots from months of cave humidity and attic dampness, you brought it to me with huge worried questions in your clear brown eyes. You presented it to me silently, opened to the many penciled lines that counted off our days in hiding. The lines, every fifth day crossed off like the gate to a picket fence, but those gates were locked to freedom. The smudged gray lines spread over endpapers, margins, chapter openers. Each line representing one more day of survival. Each line a triumph. Each line a part of me I managed to lock away.

But you do not know this. To you, it looks like I've been in prison or a mad house. To some extent, I was. I chose to keep this dark part of my history hidden from you, to keep you free of fear and worry. But that is impossible. I realize now, seeing your hurt—we do our children no good when we shield them from reality.

I trace the raised cover letters of the title—*Personal Recollections of Joan of Arc*—so familiar, like my own signature. The gold leaf on the leather worn off long ago.

I reread the passages I had carefully copied from the book onto strips of torn notebook paper, once used as bookmarks, now yellowing with age. They still hold so much meaning.

I close my eyes, and it's as if I am there again, in the dark, trying to live to see another day.

So now it is my turn to tell *you* a story, my darling daughter. My story. Finally. May it not harm you. May it feed you in some way and give you hope.

The Shtetele

They were peaceful and pleasant, those young and smoothly flowing days of ours . . . we being remote from the seat of war, but at intervals roving bands approached near enough for us to see the flush in the sky at night, which marked where they were burning some farmstead or village, and we all knew, or at least felt, that some day they would come nearer, and we should have our turn.

—COPIED BY HANNA SLIVKA FROM
"IN DOMREMY," CHAPTER V

L EEBA AND I LINK arms together, clutching each other for courage as we make the long walk home from school. We are being followed.

For the third day in a row, they throw rocks at us. "Zhidovki! Zhidovki! Zhidovki!" they chant over and over. We keep our heads down and try not to flinch when the sharp rocks sting our skin, and the word—that terrible word for *Jews*—stings our hearts. But today, as we try to get far away from the three boys, we hear other curses in Russian and Ukrainian, and look back to see our brother, Symon. He is using his sling shot to shoot them right back with their own mean weapons, hitting each of them within seconds.

They run off.

Symon tells us he was following us quietly, out of sight, after Leeba had come home crying the day before, and he had seen me blustering about the sheep pens, kicking the weathered gray wood posts and muttering about what I would like to do to the three bullies.

Symon brags a lot. He likes to put his thumbs under his suspenders and lord it about the farm. But Leeba and I don't care. We know that under all the bragging, he has a good heart. We know he will always stand up for us.

In these early days, before the war days, life as a very young child in Kwasova is good and simple. We love the festivals that take place in our *shtetele*, and the daily rituals, tasks, and prayer time. It is a settled life for us all, but you can see it isn't perfect. What life with human beings ever is?

In Kwasova, we are part of a Jewish community in a small town made up of Galician people who were originally Russian, Polish, and Ukrainian. The name "Ukraine" means "borderland," and our country's borders keep changing. Our government keeps changing. Papa says it is because Ukraine has no natural defenses—our land is too flat.

Because of this flat land, and because we grow so much food and because rulers want our rich soil, we are at different periods in history Ukrainian citizens, then Austrian, then Polish.

We are Polish on September 1, 1939, when Hitler invades from the west, with thousands of tanks on land and planes overhead. A week after Rosh Hashanah, the Red Army marches into Kwasova from the east, singing folk songs and speaking Ukrainian, and holding off the German advance . . . and we are suddenly Russian Ukrainians, forced to pledge our allegiance to Comrade Josef Stalin. A new border is made down the middle of Poland.

The Russian flag, solid red with its hammer and sickle and star, now has replaced the Polish red and white one. Some storekeepers, too cheap to pay for a new flag, ripped the white bar off the top of their Polish flags and hung the bottom red bar. The flags flap around, tattered, making the *shtetele* look a little run down. Street signs with well-known Polish names on them are taken down.

Mama and Papa work hard to help us understand each new law, even those that try to erase our Jewish heritage. They try to keep us proud of who we are, even when we are sometimes called names.

When my parents first arrived over the border in 1927, the people of Kwasova befriended them. After all, our Ashkenazi ancestors have been on this land for almost a thousand years. And in this small, isolated valley, Jews lived side by side for hundreds of years with farmers and villagers and townspeople, even on the same street. There is no *di Yidishe gas,* no separate Jewish quarter, as there is in some towns. We even share the Ukrainian Community Hall for our Jewish dances and parties.

But a small group of Poles and Russians still view us as *zhidy,* people to be ridiculed or avoided, like the Romani gypsies who are scattered across the borderlands. And their boys taunt us. So we are wary but somewhat thankful that Comrade Stalin took over our part of the country. We hear his Red Army is holding off Adolf Hitler, *Führer* of Germany, from invading. And the Russians are letting us children go to school for free. Polish children, now under German rule over the new border, have to quit after the fourth year because Hitler thinks they only need to learn how to do simple sums and be dutiful. We know better.

I do start to notice that some Kwasovians have disappeared from around our valley (the Polish school headmaster, the Russian Orthodox priest, a Ukrainian farmer we trade with), but when I ask, Mama and Papa always have a good reason for their absence. They do not tell us about the enormous taxes being levied on them. Or of the consequences of practicing our religion. They just tell us we must do so more quietly.

As good as life looks now to a young child, there is still a sense of always looking over your shoulder for something to hit you.

Spring is my favorite time in the lower steppe lands. The world becomes green again. A new green, a baby green. It glows against the *chernozem*, the black soil that gets turned over for crops. The valley is a patchwork of furrows at different angles, all ready for the seeds to be sown—wheat, sunflowers, sugar beets, barley, oats, rye, millet, buckwheat, rice, corn, cabbage—and for the potato spuds to be planted. Breezes in Kwasova are gentle. Rivers flow high and swiftly south to meet up with the Black Sea. Farmers get ready to graze their cattle and sheep on the grasslands on the outer skirts of the fields.

Beyond the fields, where new green wheat moves like water waves in wind, patches of woodlands rise up. Beyond those—smoky blue mountains I'll never get to. They send down hot winds in summer, and cold winds in winter.

In the spring, as Mama cleans the house and prepares the kitchen for Passover, I help deliver to Kwasovians some of the *pysanky* eggs my neighbor, Mrs. Petrovich, makes. They sit safely in my willow basket, cuddled by dry meadow grass and hidden under a linen. The eggs are full but fragile. Mrs. Petrovich dyes these shells, with my help, for her Christian clients, who give them to friends and family at Easter celebrations and put them in bowls on their kitchen tables to ward off evil.

On the way to drop them off, I walk by gardens blooming with lavender lilacs hanging heavy on their stems and buzzing with many gathering bees. The lilacs also grow along roadsides, on the top side of drainage ditches. I breathe in heavily the whole way. Blue barn swallows soar in the air, catching insects. They follow the ploughs churning up the soil, chasing more food. White storks, with their black bellies, build nests on cottage roofs. They gather branches and grass on top of the brick chimneys.

The fruit trees in our backyard blossom with papery-fine white petals, and baby blue and pink forget-me-nots grow wild, everywhere. Primroses and yellow kingcups and white clover pop up in the furrows of the planted fields. Red poppies wave their bright little heads amidst green grass.

Spring starts to feel different, however, in April 1940. We still wake up to the Polish Catholic church bells ringing far and wide in cool new air, the sound no longer muffled by snow and cold. But when we prepare for Passover by throwing out grains, corn, and beans (we are not allowed by custom to eat leavened bread, or *chametz* or *kitniyot*), we now have to hide what we are doing from the Russians. Even the Catholics have to hide their *pysanky*. Comrade Stalin does not like religion.

I take the heavy sack of grain up the back hill behind our home because its contents must be removed from the house and placed far away for seven days. I place the sack in a barrel under some bushes (we cannot afford to burn any food in these times, as we have on other Passovers). Then I stand and look over the valley and watch the smoke plumes from nearby cattle trains rise straight up into cloudless blue skies.

How would I know as a child that some of those cattle cars are filled with many Polish prisoners heading to Siberian gulags? The trains do not stop in Kwasova.

And I do not hear the bombs dropping in Paris. All I see, at this point in time, is the beauty of those puffing plumes. I watch the smoke reshape its storm cloud form, over and over, while I stand on the hill. The hill is the highest point in town.

Symon loves to follow Fedir Woliński, the Polish lamplighter, during his nightly rounds. Our town has no wired electricity yet, just some generators in the town halls that the NKVD, or Soviet police officers, confiscated to run their communication systems and propaganda films. Full electricity is only in the larger towns, or in cities like Lwów and Kiev. That means we need a lamplighter. Fedir the Lamplighter, we call him.

The lamplighter carries a wooden ladder and pole with a wick on the end to light the kerosene lamps on their sturdy metal poles. Most of the lights are scattered closer to the *shtetele* center, so we wander in toward the main square when we don't have schoolwork. We kick stones along the way, crossing over the small bridges that cover the drainage ditches that criss-cross Kwasova.

"My little lamplighter," Fedir says from atop his ladder, and climbs down. The ladder is only used when he needs to trim a wick or refill the oil. If a lamp is full, he hands Symon the long pole with the lit wick at the end for lighting. Symon, at eight, is big enough now that he no longer needs help to reach the lamp wick. With a look of pure purpose on his face, he guides the pole to the lamp till it catches, and the lamplight spills out and cuts into the dark that seeps around us. It bathes his little face. His blond hair glows.

When it gets late, the NKVD officers, smoking and laughing, start to leave the tavern. We are in danger of missing curfew, so Fedir the Lamplighter gives Symon a gentle nudge back in the direction of home.

"Get you to bed now, young Symon."

We rush back, trying to stay a step ahead of punishment.

The puddles of rain and daily wash water reflect the glowing yellow glass orbs our brother lit, tiny nighttime suns in the dusty path of the road that leads home.

Spring is also the time of the annual Shepherd's Parade. But the last one our *shtetele* holds is in 1941. Papa and others have to convince the Russians we can have it.

Papa is a smart man, as Mama loves to say when he does something that makes her proud of him. She tugs on his wiry black beard and calls him a *yidishn kop*. He makes sure he is on friendly terms with Commissar Egorov, who heads the small group of NKVD officers now stationed in the town hall. The NKVD search for rebellious partisan fighters who hide in the forests, and for Polish nationalists who give them trouble. They are trying to "Sovietize" us, as our teachers say.

Papa has two jobs. He is a sheepherder. He inherited the sheep when he bought the land we live on, and he decided to keep them. Symon loves the sheep, gives them belly rubs, and loves the large shaggy sheepdog, Ovid, that herds them.

Papa's second job is to fix things. He fixes the Russians' old, broken-down army trucks when no one else can. Because the Russians need him, they listen to him. When the local farmers come to him, asking him to help them petition the Russians to allow them to hold their annual parade, which the Russians banned because they see it as a religious event, he joins them to convince the commissar it is a community celebration that could be held in honor of Comrade Stalin.

It works.

Papa assigns Leeba the task of sewing a long red banner from cloth that the commissar's wife is to bring from Russia. Because we have to wait for the wife and the cloth, the parade is moved to June, rather than being held in the traditional month of May.

JUNE 22, 1941 —

We are excited when parade day finally arrives. Papa leaves early to get his wagon decorated. I help Mama prepare a Sunday breakfast of plain *blinis* by mixing the wheat flour batter. We rarely get the sugar and potted cream anymore that she used to serve with them, before the Russians came. The Red Army, which had marched into town as ragged, hungry soldiers, smelling of alcohol and singing, ate most of our food and drank most of our liquor. They left us with little, and the shopkeepers are still having trouble replacing their wares. Food on the shelves is stale, the salt dirty, the matches cheap and hard to light.

Mama makes sure Symon always gets extra food. "He is a growing boy," she says, and my sister and I kick him under the table to tease him. Symon kicks back.

"When will I be able to ride in the wagon?" he asks.

The parade is a formal march of sheep and cattle herders, and only those old enough to herd get to ride in it.

"Let me see, you are nine years old, my *babka*. You still have a few years left in primary school before you can go out into the grasslands alone. Don't be in such a rush," Mama says. She waves a forkful of *blini* at him. "School is better. Out there, nothing to stretch your mind. Just wind and grass and smelly sheep."

Papa used to sell the sheep's wool directly to local wool mills and milliners, and sometimes lambs to the local Jewish butcher. Osip the Butcher, we call him. As I said, Papa is also the local repairman. In his barn workshop, he repairs anything that moves, or anything that has stopped and needs to move again—objects like watches, wagon wheels, churns, guns, and animal traps. We have no guns in our home—Papa is against them—but there are those who hunt, and they rely on their firearms to eat. So Papa is considered an important man in town, especially now that he can speak to the commissar. Papa owns a solid brick house on a lane that leads to the grazing meadows, with only one other thatched cottage on that lane. The cottage belongs to Mrs. Petrovich, my friend and employer across the street. She sold her land to Papa when he and Mama moved to Kwasova.

"I want to be with smelly sheep," Symon mutters.

The walk to the center of town is only a mile. The families gather in front of the public square, and someone plays a *buben* and a few Kwasovians dance. Today, everyone dances together, instead of in their separate community halls, celebrating life renewed. Then someone rings a church bell and the parade starts with the ringing of smaller bells on the horses' manes and harnesses and on the wood wagons. Down the cobbled street they come, jangling and jingling and prancing, as if the horses know everyone is looking at them. The carts have some prize sheep on them for show, and the few herders who are left, who have not been sent away by the Red Army, wave and yell to those they know. The wagon wheels, cleaned of rust so they will not make noise as they turn, shine in bright sunlight.

Leeba's banner is held at either end by two pretty girls in embroidered Russian dresses. They march at the front of the parade with serious faces, the same serious way we had seen the Russian soldiers march in their propaganda films, which glow blue on the screen on those nights we are forced to watch them in the town hall.

Mama pats Leeba's head proudly. Her brown hair is shiny and pulled tightly into two pigtails. Her cheeks are always rosy. My hair is usually a messy blond bob. I reach up and pat it down as it blows in the wind.

Some boys in the crowd whoop and holler. They are wearing hats made of large green squash leaves, to keep the hot sun from burning their fair cheeks and noses. Some men have tucked brilliant-colored rooster feathers into their worn hats to dress them up.

Across the way, I see my friend Leon Stadnick. His face is grim. It is a face I know well. I study it closely whenever we meet in the square or at dances. I like his face because there is often a smile on it that creates a dimple in his left cheek. The dimple is not there now, though. He seems to be staring off into the distance. He is looking beyond the parade and the revelers, into the distant hills. I wave, try to catch his attention. But he doesn't react. Embarrassed, I drop my hand and glance side to side to see if anyone noticed.

Symon smirks up at me. I slap his hand.

"There's Papa!" Leeba cries, and the hand she is letting rest in mine pulls away to wave. She jumps up and down. Papa hears her and smiles down at her as he passes, and Mama blows him a kiss. He pretends to catch it and put it to his heart. He looks very handsome, with his trimmed black beard and new felt hat. Then he winks and rides out of sight.

My sister Leeba came into this world two winters after I was born. I was happy. She was round, with chubby red cheeks and pudgy balls of hands that wrapped around my finger if I placed it just right. When her little fingers curled so hard around mine, I felt like I was part of something bigger than myself.

Symon was born two years after Leeba. He gave my parents trouble from the start. He wouldn't come out, Mama said. At least, not in the way he was supposed to, head first. The midwife needed all her skill to turn him around, as Symon was trying hard to come out with his feet. Mrs. Petrovich, who had watched over me in our kitchen the day Leeba was born, shuffled us off quickly to her house to be away from the "ordeal," as she called it. Leeba and I held hands, dodging muddy puddles in the dirt and gravel road. I wondered if this new baby's problem was that it was not born in winter as we had been, but in summer.

But he and Mama made it through the "ordeal."

After Leeba was born, before Symon came, Papa saved enough money to build our brick house. It was topped with a shingled roof, built a few hundred feet away from the two-room cabin I was born in. Not many houses outside of town had shingled roofs. Most were thatched. And most had walls of painted wooden boards or logs and plaster, not solid bricks. I remember when the house was done, I was so excited to have stairs to climb to bed. It made going to sleep more of an adventure.

Because Papa has the kind of mind that can fix anything, and he is head of a special artisans' association, people come to the house for advice. Tonight, I hear the Cohan twins arrive, then Mr. Rabinowitz with Mr. Stadnick, Leon's father. Mama sometimes leaves the men to drink and talk while she mends clothes upstairs, but tonight she is still downstairs, and lets my uncle Levi in, too. I know all their voices as well as I know Papa's.

I like being awake as much as possible, and I hate sleeping. I often pinch myself and keep my eyes open as long as I can, way after Leeba turns over and Symon starts his quiet snore across the room. But on this night in late June, I do not need to pinch myself. I am very awake. I have too much energy left in me from the parade excitement. And it is unusually quiet. It isn't the raised voices in friendly debate over the Talmud or *shtetele* laws or association politics, with much chair scraping and glass clinking, which is how these gatherings usually go.

My ears prick up, as ears do, when other voices are being quiet on purpose. I decide to creep to the head of the stairs, avoiding squeaky floorboards, to hear why.

It is the young Cohan brothers who are talking. The twins have a way of communicating that is all their own. Orphaned during the hunger war, they grew up with help from our *shtetele*, staying in barns for short periods and working for meals. They were once our water carriers. Now they have their own horse and wagon and a room with the local Ukrainian dairy farmer, Stepan Illiouk. The commissar, who likes his sweets, gave the twins special travel permits. If anyone wants their goods delivered to another town or village, or a trade done, you hire the Cohans. They are strong and stocky, can carry anything, and can bargain with the stingiest customers.

Since Comrade Stalin has taken our radios and newspapers away, the twins are now also our news bearers. I hear them talking rapidly.

"This new war is not just in Poland now," Pavel says.

"Adolf Hitler's army has defied Comrade Stalin and crossed the border early this morning in a surprise attack," Jacob says.

"War is in our country now."

"Comrade Stalin has been blocking all news of the German invasion. Ukrainians are welcoming the Germans. They remember how civilized they were during the last time they invaded and hope they will free us from Russia and again sponsor independence in Ukraine."

"But those were different soldiers, aristocrats. These soldiers are more common and don't follow the rules of war. German tanks are just rolling over the planted fields, crushing crops, followed by the attacking army with automatic machine guns. Their Luftwaffe are bombing airfields. We heard they are beginning to round up Jews and force them to work in ghettoes or factories, or are deporting them."

"I hear they are telling other Jews that they are going to the Land of Israel for resettlement."

A few moments of silence. The echo of Papa's knuckles rapping against wood. One sign he is thinking hard on something.

"How far away are they?" Papa asks.

"They are north of us right now," Pavel answers.

"They are attacking Lwów."

"And they are coming west of us, from Hungary. It is hard to know yet if we are in the direct path."

Uncle Levi adds, "I am sure the Red Army will stop them soon, it is so large. Our country is so large. There is no surprise any longer. Their army cannot cover every valley."

"And we are so far away at this point, the army has time to mobilize," Mr. Stadnick says.

"But the NKVD evacuated during the parade! They used the parade to hide their departure. We broke the prison locks and let the political prisoners they were holding go a few hours ago." Pavel finishes with anger, "Those who were still alive. They shot most of them in retreat."

"The Red Army is fleeing, not fighting," Jacob adds.

"The commissar is gone?" Papa asks incredulously.

"Yes."

There is silence for a few moments. Then Mama asks, "What if the Germans come up from Romania?"

More silence. I feel dread growing in my curling toes. It moves up to my heart, which starts pounding. Are we in danger? Would they want to take us away from our home? Or worse? Kwasova is near the border of Romania. Where would we go? We could not go west to Poland, nor north into Russia, nor east into the Sea of Azov.

Papa's calm voice ends the talk. "There is nothing we can do right now, except keep our eyes and ears open and be prepared. Pavel, Jacob, we need you now more than ever. Even if you have nothing to deliver, I will pay you every week to go around the steppes, gathering news. Are you willing to do that?"

The young men murmur yeses. I scamper back to bed as I can hear my mother's feet starting toward the stairs. Under the sheet, I move closer to Leeba's night warmth. Even though it is summer outside, I am chilled and I want her near. Her night shift is damp from perspiration and she smells of grass and the fading lilacs she was playing with today. I nuzzle the lace around her collar and breathe her in. "I won't let anyone take you away," I whisper.

Symon snorts of a sudden in his sleep, as if to say, *What about me?*

"You neither," I whisper to his vague form across the room.

That parade day was our last time of true merriment and some comfort. From then on, Hitler and his approaching army invade our world. In school, children ask what the word *führer* means. The teachers say it means "leader." That there are good leaders and bad ones. And that this German one is a bad one.

Under the stern posters of Lenin and Stalin, our teachers struggle to keep us feeling safe while they try to tell the truth and answer other hard questions. Not that they know much more than we do. Around this time, the distance between Jews and other Kwasovians widens. Some adults, not just the young bullies, stare and whisper as we pass by now. In the few stores that are still open and offer meagre supplies, the Ukrainian shopkeepers make us pay in Russian rubles, worth more now than our own Polish *złotych*, or they make us trade instead of giving us the credit we are accustomed to receiving.

From my bed at night, I hear nothing more that summer from below (maybe Mama caught a glimpse of my retreating white gown as she climbed the stairs). But the Cohan brothers stop by in late afternoon or evening, many times, and we are always shooed outside.

Evenings fading into dusk and dark are magical in Kwasova. You can't help but enjoy the end of the day. The tang of rotting fruit in the clear air is carried on night breezes from orchards and backyard gardens. The lone wolf howls from the distant mountain ranges. The pack of wolves howl together when they are talking to each other. The quiet cricket song. The acidic, musky smell of neighbors' cookfires. Before the Russians came and food was bountiful, you could tell what was being cooked, our different customs getting all mixed up together in the night air—fragrant Jewish *cholent* stews, made with meat, beans, and barley, and fragrant yeasty Ukrainian *pampushy* skillet rolls.

During harvest time, we also once celebrated the joyous holiday of Sukkōt. We built small shepherd-like huts in the amber fields, sprinkled with tall haystacks. We ate or slept in the *sukkah* and gave thanks for the harvest and commemorated our ancestors' years of desert wandering. Celebrating in the huts with roofs built from brush that grows from the ground reminded us of how God gave protection in the wilderness. The temporary *sukkah* glowed under the setting sun, as did all the field haystacks, which made the whole world look gold. Even the air, after the fields were threshed, was a liquid gold from wheat and hay dust, speckled with the dark shapes of migrating birds and squawking geese.

This year, 1941, we have to celebrate in the house, curtains drawn.

Soon, snow blankets the steppes, wind whistles down from the mountains and pushes its way into cracks around doors and windows. As Kwasovians keep more to their cottages, stoking their stoves with coal and with wood gathered in fall, news and the Cohan brothers' visits seem to slow. While Hitler's army, the Wehrmacht, have already captured our country, they have not made it to Kwasova. They crossed just north and south of our tiny valley, headed west.

Perhaps the snow is keeping the German military at bay, too. Maybe even evil makes less progress in the cold?

FEBRUARY 22, 1942—

My fourteenth birthday dawns in a flurry of thick snow-flakes. "Just like on the day you were born," Mama says, giving me the special heart-shaped *blinis* she makes for each of our birthdays. She'd made mine the day before the Sabbath, and warmed them up this morning on the iron stove. Mrs. Petrovich had been over earlier to light it for us.

I slather on Mama's tart homemade blackberry jam and sprinkle on about a quarter spoon of powdered sugar. She'd saved the last scrapings for me from the bottom of the sugar crock. There is no more to be had in Kwasova. The sugar looks like snow against dark soil. She gives me fresh, heavy breakfast cream skimmed from the top of our cow's milk, in her best flowered cup. Later, we will open presents with Mrs. Petrovich.

On Saturday, the Sabbath, the Torah commands we rest. We cannot use matches or machinery or unlock doors or cook and labor, so a non-Jew must help out and strike the matches or turn the keys for us. Our closest neighbor, Mrs. Petrovich, is our Shabbes goy. With her help, we can still have heat in the winter and lock the front door at night. Since the NKVD took our floor carpets, the rooms are draftier and the stove's heat is even more crucial. Mrs. Petrovich refuses payment, but now and then accepts a jar of Mama's fruit preserves, and my help.

Since it is Saturday, I don't have to go to school, and I am excited to have a full day to celebrate for the first time in five years. After the service at synagogue, we had said our blessings and began our first Sabbath meal.

"I made you something," Leeba says, smiling at me, shaking her pigtails.

Symon frowns, hating to be left out.

"She spent many hours on it." Mama nods her approval. Our mother is a great worker. Papa always says it is why he married her. He's never known a woman who worked harder. He wanted an equal partner, he told his matchmaker, and she'd known just the right young woman for him—Leonid Kaidanov's girl, Eva—my mother. Leeba is just like her, better at sitting still and concentrating than I am, and wonderful with a needle and thread and knitting tools, so she is given more praise from our mother. I try not to let it bother me. Mostly, it doesn't.

"I made some—" Symon starts to compete, but he stops abruptly when we hear a wagon pull up in the lane outside our front door. We run to the windows. The horses stamp their feet, snorting breath that mists the air. Their manes are heavy with frozen icicles. Voices and chains and harnesses and ice jangle.

Mama opens the door. Snow blows in like white road dust when Pavel enters with the frozen air. He grabs her arm and pulls her aside, whispering into her ear. I see her face go as white as the snow on his shoulders.

"You must get Abram," she says. "I do not know what to do."

He nods. "Can I take your horse? Mine need to cool down."

"Yes, and take them around back and put them in the barn for now." I see the efficient mother come back. Her voice is stronger now and her face has color again.

She lets Pavel out the door, and we hear the wagon wheels turn into the side yard. We abandon our farm chairs and rush to the windows to look out. Nothing special, just Jacob guiding the horses and the wagon covered with snow-laden blankets into the barn. Disappointed, we sit down and finish eating.

While we eat the heart-shaped *blinis*, Mama bustles about. She gathers the extra wool blankets we use in the main room downstairs when we are cold and the big black iron coal stove doesn't throw enough heat. She folds the blankets carefully, then opens her cupboards and stares into each one. Now and then she takes something out—stale chunks of bread she uses for breadcrumbs, Mrs. Umański's pot cheese in a crock, and dried apple slices from our garden. As she wraps these in a towel, Papa enters. She falls into his arms, bundle and all, and starts crying.

We go quiet. We have never seen her cry, not even when she had Symon. I hold my breath, waiting for Papa to fix something I didn't even know was broken.

"It's just for one night," he soothes her. "How can we turn them away?"

"What's happening?" Symon asks, tugging on Papa's pant leg.

"We have guests, Symon, but they are secret guests. You are not to tell anyone they are here. Do you understand? Not anyone. It would be bad for them. And for us." He looks pointedly at me, and I know he is thinking of Mrs. Petrovich. But he doesn't know her like I do. Doesn't know she would never give us up.

"But why us?" Mama asks.

"Because we are so far out. We only have one neighbor who might see what is happening." Papa picks up the blankets and food bundle and heads back out the door. "Just one night, remember?" he throws back at Mama, as he closes the door behind him.

We all stare at its knotted boards for a few moments.

"All right, children." The no-nonsense Mama has returned once again. She claps her hands. "Time to clean up and go out and play. But only in the street today, do you hear me? Not in the back . . ."

We put on our thick wool *kurtkas* and our leather boots and wool hats and mittens and tumble out into the swirling white world. I stand in the front lane, face up to the sky. *I am fourteen today*, I say to myself. The sky drops its feathery frozen wetness on my face and body, like its own gift. The world felt so still yesterday, but today, it all seems to be moving around us again. Who is in the barn? I wonder. And if they would bring badness to us, why is Papa letting them stay?

Leeba and Symon run around, throwing snowballs at each other. Maybe because it is my birthday, I feel much older than they are at this moment.

Mrs. Petrovich always joins us for my birthday apple cake and the gift giving, at my request. Today, I get a pretty new dress that Mama has cut down and fashioned from her own old gingham dress—with a daisy pattern and yellow porcelain buttons. Comrade Stalin does not allow his people more than one change of clothes. We were told he believes it is a bad thing to have too many possessions, but Mama hid this one under her mattress when the clothes and furs were confiscated, knowing that later she would remake it for my birthday. Gifts are important on birthdays, as they ward off evil for the year.

Leeba gives me a long scarf she'd knitted in reds and browns, because I lost my old one, and Symon gives me a shiny red rock from his collection and a wooden box he made to put it in. Mrs. Petrovich waits for all the gifts to be given, then pulls me over to her chair and puts an arm around me. She hands me a package wrapped in brown paper, the kind of paper we used to get around our meat at Osip the Butcher's store, before he was not allowed to sell kosher meat and he was forced to close. I unfold the stiff flaps and find a beautiful new white apron with small embroidered eggs around the edges in pinks and greens.

"That is for you to wear when you come to help me. I'll keep it for you by the door." I kiss her on her soft, powdery cheek, knowing Mama is probably frowning because she does not like me working on the eggs Mrs. Petrovich decorates.

After she leaves and we go to bed upstairs, I wait for Papa to come home and join us on the second floor. The front door opens and closes. He takes a long time. The light from the kerosene lantern still flickers, sending bouncing shadows up the stairwell. I can't sleep, thinking of the mystery in the barn, so I get out of bed, careful not to wake Leeba, put on some socks, and tiptoe downstairs. Papa is looking at a map on the broad kitchen table.

I sit down across from him and he looks up. Smiling gently, he reaches out for my hand. I put it on the table in the space between us and he takes it and holds it in his palm, caressing it, looking at it in wonder. "You are a young woman now, Hanna. When did that happen?"

"Papa, can you tell me who is in the barn? I promise I won't tell anyone."

He is quiet for a few moments, continuing to caress my hand with a large callused thumb. He strokes his long beard with his other hand. He does this when he is thinking hard on something. Then he sighs, lets my hand go, sits back, and points to a place on the map near the bottom of the paper, to Romania.

"This is where they come from," he explains, "and this is where they are going." He moves his hand to the top of the map, to his right. "They are nameless. They are people like us. They are fleeing for their lives, trying to make it to a safe place in the north. They have a long, perilous journey. . . ." He sighs again. "Pavel and Jacob were stopped by a farmer they knew a few towns away. He had these people in his barn. He entrusted our young twins with this family. And they, in turn, entrusted the family to us for the night. They will be gone before you wake in the morning, and no one will be in the barn tomorrow. That is all you need to know."

I listen, eyes wide. A whole family in our barn? Fleeing for their lives? I think of the cold barn, the lack of heat, wind whistling down from the mountains and through the drafty boards, the miles they still have to travel. I creep back upstairs and open my trunk, then climb back down.

"Papa, can you take this to them before they leave? Leeba gave it to me today." It is so soft. I reluctantly hand him the new scarf, knowing I will never see it again. Papa takes it from my hands, flattens the folded wool, and looks back up at me. Sorrow pools in his gentle brown eyes.

"Hanna, my Hanna, you *are* growing up."

He gets up from the table and walks to the hanging book-shelf over the sofa. He takes down a leather-bound book with gilded pages, brushes his hand across the cover. "You are old enough to read this now."

He hands it to me. *Personal Recollections of Joan of Arc,* by Mark Twain. *What a funny name,* I think. I have never owned an adult book before. I run my finger over the em-bossed cover with joy. The NKVD had confiscated all our re-ligious books, including Mama's Yiddish *Tsenerene,* and most of our Ukrainian and Polish literature books, seeing them as anti-Soviet. But Papa had talked the commissar into letting him keep a small shelf of fiction books by American and European writers that didn't threaten the communist regime. In return, for Papa, Mama swallowed her anger and made the commissar a green hat with a red feather in it, after hearing from the local seamstress that Commissar Egorov had a taste for Polish hats. The seamstress said he had bought up each *kapelusz* for men at the dry goods store when he'd first arrived.

Papa gives me a long hug, then leaves through the rear door.

Back in bed, I finally feel like I can drift off, knowing someone will be a bit warmer tonight. Maybe even a girl my own age. But before I close my eyes, I take another look at my new book, translated into Polish. The preface by Mr. Twain describes this real woman from the past, this Joan of Arc. It says her century "was the brutalist, the wickedest, the rottenest in history since the dark ages." But somehow Joan stayed honest, modest, and honorable.

I wonder if Papa is sending me a private message. I stow the book carefully under my bed.

It happens during a few more spring and summer days. The wagon pulls up. If Leeba and Symon and I are inside, we avoid the windows. If we are outside, we go into the house. I send my brother and sister upstairs and help Mama gather up supplies that Auntie Maya, her sister in town, has donated in the event it happens again. Mama no longer needs Papa home. She knows what to do. And so do I.

Until late summer, when two ragged boys are dropped off by the farmer Stepan Illiouk. It is not part of our routine.

Mama stands in the doorway, shaking, when I come in from picking garden blackberries, purple juice on my fingertips. It is a beautiful August day, and I had been taking my time, poking around the bramble bushes, looking for the darkest globes of fruit.

"Why are you bringing them here?" she asks the farmer.

"Not to worry, Eva. I know what the Cohans are doing. I found these boys in my fields, eating beet greens. They will tell you their story. I have to get back before someone asks where I have gone to." He snaps his reins and whistles and the wagon takes off, leaving the two dark-haired boys staring at us, and we at them.

Mama hesitates only for an instant. Then she steps off the stoop and guides them quickly to the back of the house and to the barn. This time, I follow. She doesn't make me go back.

"What are your names?" she asks.

They just stare at her.

"I can't help you if you don't give me some information. You can trust us." She pauses. "We are Jewish, too."

They look at each other, and it's as if some silent message gets passed between them.

They say they are from a group of young Jewish saboteurs from Lwów, which is now fully occupied. So far they have managed to hide out in the back of a printer's shop. The saboteurs do small things to hurt the Germans: rip down their flags, write graffiti on walls, start small fires in their warehouses. They had finally been caught after the last fire.

"We were put on a train," the one with curly brown hair says.

"We knew what that meant," the one with straight black hair says. "When the train slowed down, we jumped out a small window and walked south."

"We walked as far as we could at night. We were very hungry, so we stopped to eat the beet greens, and that is when the farmer found us."

"He said we should go to his priest, who used to help run the Ukrainian Catholic church in town. This priest is baptizing Jews and making new birth certificates for them. He said, 'Father Dubrowski knows what to do with children,' but that he could not take us himself."

"Hanna, go get some bread while I try to figure out what to do."

I go into the house, put down the berry basket, and hesitate. We have a half loaf of brown bread. There is not much left. It is the first time I am a bit hesitant to help. We need food, too. But they have been so brave.

I say out loud, "Shame on you, Hanna," and put two thick slabs in a wood bowl and take it to the barn. Just then Symon comes in from the fields, and Mama sends him with a note to get Auntie Maya. By the time he brings her back, it will likely be getting dark.

Mama and I wait in the kitchen, nervous, drumming our fingers on the table and doing small chores to keep our minds off this new problem. Leeba is upstairs, sick with a cold. We leave her alone. A dry cough can be heard now and then.

When you are afraid of something outside of yourself, all your senses get stronger. Both Mama and I hear a muffled rustling at the front door while we wash dishes. We stare at each other, eyes wide. It is too soon for Symon.

Then, a knock.

Mama is frozen. She looks at me in panic. I put down my washing rag and walk slowly to the door, unlock it, and push down the handle.

Mrs. Petrovich is already walking back to her cottage. She had quietly left a basket of fresh chicken eggs on our stoop. Mama shakes her head when she pulls back the linen napkin and sees the green and brown and white eggs, and I smile at the proof of our friendship.

"I suppose she saw the boys, and thinks she knows what is happening in our barn," she says. "It is hard to hide things from neighbors. We are lucky she is your friend and did not go to the Ukrainian police. They are now collaborating with the Nazis."

We clean off the waste and the tiny down feathers and boil the eggs in a pan of water. Then we pack half a dozen damp, warm eggs into a bundle. I feel good knowing these eggs will feed and keep two half-starved little heroes alive.

Auntie Maya comes back, with Symon and Papa, in our wagon, just as the sun appears large and is starting to move down in the sky, highlighting the tops of trees.

"I thought someone was hurt!" she says, when Mama tells her why she'd requested the bandages. Papa listens to Mama murmur something into his ear, and nods in agreement.

"Yes, that will work."

I walk with Mama and Auntie Maya to the barn. The boys are in their hiding place, bits of egg shells scattered around them where they sit hunched over. I wonder, did they eat the shells, too?

"Come out," Mama orders.

She takes the curly-haired one. My aunt takes the straight-haired one. I cut the bandages and hand the cloth to them and they both wind the strips around the dark heads, the jaws, and the center of the boys' faces, below the eyes. When they're done, they look like wounded little soldiers.

She puts a hand on each of their arms, then speaks firmly.

"If anyone asks, you two were hurt during a farm accident. You are to keep these on till you are in a safe place. Because you cannot hide your Jewish identity, the priest will be unable to get you adopted, so he will have to find a safe house for you. I am guessing he will teach you Catholic prayers in the event someone gets suspicious and asks you to recite some, but until then, you are strangers in this *shtetele* and, hence, will be seen with suspicion and will not be protected, so stay inside."

They nod, their dark eyes, wide and serious, about the only part of their faces you can see. They are about Symon's age.

Why anyone would hurt them is so hard for me to understand. That they have to hide a part of who they are to live is even harder to accept. They remind me of Leeba. I shudder to think of the same people coming after her.

Papa says they can't risk taking them to the priest until the sun goes down completely. He has to take them under cover of darkness. He can't risk taking the wagon, either, which would make noise after curfew.

They wait for the clouds to cover the sliced curl of a moon, and leave by foot. From the bedroom window, I watch. They are small shadows disappearing into the fields. Could I be as brave as they had been in enacting their small sabotages against a huge evil army?

I'm not sure.

Eventually even Leeba and Symon came to understand what was happening in the barn, but they knew the consequences, which were now imprisonment, or even death, so kept quiet. Except for those two boys, we never met those who passed the night in the barn, never saw a single one. Not a hair, not a hand. Like invisible souls, they melted in and out of our lives in just twenty-four hours. Papa took care of the one thing they left behind, in a slop bucket. He mixed it in with the horse waste so he wouldn't be caught going from the barn to the outhouse with human waste. We still had friends and clients who stopped by, asking for or bringing items for repair.

We will never find out if they survived their journeys or not. All we have is hope that some will, and a good feeling that we might be saving lives.

Soon, the wagon stops bringing its precious loads. The borders are closed. The Wehrmacht soldiers have multiplied and expanded in force and are spreading out into the valleys. And there is a unit so terrible it is only discussed in whispers. That task force is called the Einsatzgrüppen. Even worse than the German army are the "clean-up" crews. Some follow the Wehrmacht advance with guns and killer dogs, and some follow with gas vans and classical music.

It is too late to flee ourselves. Jews are no longer able to leave Europe.

We hold our breath. . . .

The few girls my age in town are Catholic Poles and they no longer go to school. Their parents don't think the girls need more education. They keep to themselves, which means I've never had a girlfriend. My sister is my closest friend. After that, there is Leon, a year older. As Jews, we learn our culture in different ways. Before the Russians came, the boys learned the Talmud at Hebrew school, while we girls mixed with the other groups at the seven-year public school. We learned Polish when the Poles were in charge and then Russian languages and doctrines when the Russians were in charge. When the Russians closed the Hebrew schools, the boys joined us, too.

Now, since the Russians abandoned the *shtetele*, the teachers have gone back to teaching in Polish.

This is one reason why I like Leon Stadnick. When I go back to my seven-year primary school in the fall and we break for lunch outside, Leon comes over to talk to me from the temporary school across the street. It is no longer safe for the older boys to go to the *gymnazium* up north (Jews were being ordered not to attend school in the cities), so our *shtetele* quickly set up a small private secondary school in the abandoned hat store.

As the oldest girl at my school, I mostly just sit and read by myself while the others play.

So when Leon comes over, I feel noticed. He is different from the rest of the boys, who play rough games and curse and tumble about. He shows me drawings in his school notebooks, in the margins, careful not to let anyone else see. We sit with our backs against an ancient, gnarly oak tree with a thick trunk, which shields us from view. I read and he draws.

He flips the pages slowly. Usually I see carefully etched lines in pencil of the small things that fill our world, things that no one else much notices. Like the new glasses Avrum, one of the students, is now wearing, or the roundish stones and the grassy weeds in our schoolyard, or the flies that get in through the open windows and become part of the background noise. Those kinds of things.

But today when he shows me his drawings, I become quiet. Crooked cross flags with bullet holes ripped into them, planes dropping dark runnels of bombs to the bottom of the pages, and areas on the paper where he had just gone in circles with his pencil, leaving a soft, shiny dark place.

These leaden circles look like the half circles under his eyes.

The market square has changed. It used to be bustling with tinkers and gypsies and local peasants selling their wares, calling out mostly in Polish and Yiddish. In front of rows of dry goods stores, leather stores, a drug store, and several butcher stores and bakeries, fruits and vegetables and candies spilled out of kiosks and handmade wheelbarrows made from wooden fruit boxes. The smells were both intoxicating and nasty. Spices and onions and garlic mixed with yeast and sugar and woodsy smoke and the rotten tang of animal manure. Voices called out greetings, and I remember loud clanging from the blacksmith forge, the clopping of horses' hooves and the grinding of iron wheels on rounded cobblestones, and laughter and organ music.

But now, the market has only one bakery with long lines, one dairy shop, one butcher who is not allowed to sell kosher meat, just what little fresh meat he can get, and one dry goods store. My uncle, who is a cobbler, was forced to give up his shoe and leather shop when the Russians came.

All the shopkeepers are Ukrainian now. No more Jewish bakers making flat *matzoh* for Passover or braided *challah* for the Sabbath. No one travels from the valley to the market on weekends to sell anything beyond old musty used clothing and shoes. Black marketers knock on doors at night to sell their stolen or traded contraband at prices few can afford. The local police issue ration cards so what little food is available can be stretched to feed Kwasova, especially bread.

Mama comes back from the market one fall day while I am churning milk for butter, and I hear her yelling in the barn, where Papa is working. Mama never yells. I poke my head out the back door and hear something about "posters" and "clothes off their dead backs." When she comes back inside and slams down her willow basket, it is empty. I stay silent.

"I can't go to the market any longer, Hanna, I have to send you on weekends. With your blond hair, you may get more from those bloodsuckers."

"What happened?"

"I got there early to be first in line." Mama paces back and forth. "Before the doors opened, a Ukrainian policeman I didn't recognize came up to me and asked me what my name was and to see my ration card. When I said 'Eva Slivka' and showed him my card, he pulled me out of line and put me last. By the time I got to the counter, there was no bread left."

It is getting harder to get flour to make our own kosher bread, so these rations are very important to us.

Papa, now at the open front door, wipes grease from his hands on a rag, then touches the *mezuzah* outside and lightly kisses his fingers. He ducks his head under the doorframe. "We can't rely on this bread ration. I'll see if Ivan will trade us a bit of flour for some apples. I do not like dealing with the Polish black market. They'll take everything we own."

We all stare down long and hard at the empty basket, as if we are in a dark fairy tale and something might magically appear.

That week, at school, I notice the Polish students sitting a distance away from the Jewish girls and whispering and looking at us sideways.

On Saturday, Mama wakes me when the night is just losing its hold on darkness and the stars are fading. I rub my eyes, reluctant to leave the warm bed.

She gives me the basket and the small ration card, brushes her hand over my wavy bobbed hair, then lifts my chin with her fingers and looks into my eyes. Hers are brown, with gold specks in them, surrounded by beautiful long lashes that curl on their own. I know them so well.

"You will see things I don't want you to see, but we need to feed so many mouths. Hold your head up high and ask for more."

The walk to the market square is lonely at this time of morning. I feel tense with anticipation, wondering what is ahead of me. Crickets chirp briefly, slow and cold as I am in the cool air. Bats fly back to their nesting places. I listen to the sound of my leather shoes scuffing and crunching along the dirt road.

When I get to the market square, and pass by many empty storefronts, the shopkeepers are beginning to open the few stores that are still active. The bakery is still closed, though. Just a small group of six women wait in line in the street leading up to the front wooden steps. I will not be first today, but I will still be in a good position.

I take my place behind them with my ration card for 2 ounces of bread. They are speaking Polish, talking about lice. I tune them out and stamp my feet for warmth on the cobblestones. The line behind me grows longer and the air warms as the sun continues to rise high in the sky. I stop shivering, but I keep looking around for the Ukrainian policeman who had confronted Mama.

When the bakers open the double wood doors, their bells overhead ring from the movement, and the line starts to surge forward. It is then that I see what the women had been talking about, and why the schoolchildren had stopped sitting near us Jews—against the grimy left front display window is a new, colorful poster. In red Polish letters, which look like they were painted on with a brush, it reads: BEWARE OF TYPHUS. AVOID JEWS.

In the center of the poster is a drawing of an elderly man, who looks like he is a Russian Bukharan Jew, wearing flowing blue-black robes and spectacles and their traditional pill box *yarmulke* cap. A long beard and mustache hang low, weighing down his sad face. He has *huge* oversized skeletal hands. To his right is a blue Mogen Dovid, a Jewish star; to the left of him, a purple skull. All over his robe are crawling larger-than-life pinkish lice.

On the right display window is another poster, all words: THE JEW, INCITER OF WAR, PROLONGER OF WAR.

The women in front of me say something about the posters being from Lwów.

This must be what Mama was talking about, I think. I can't help but brush off my dress, as if I were brushing off the pink lice, and I hold my head up higher, as the woman behind me backs away, leaving extra space between us. I recognize her, and I know she recognizes me—she knows I am the daughter of Abram Slivka, who fixes her husband's hay scales. My stomach churns and my face grows red. I have the self-protective urge to slap her. But I can't. She might turn me in to the Ukrainian policeman, who is now stationed on the sidewalk, watching the line.

Is he the same one who pulled Mama aside?

I begin to sweat. Beads form on my forehead and my armpits grow damp and I need to pee. It feels like forever until we make it up the stairs and inside the shop, past the rifle-carrying policeman who glances right over my blond bob without a question. The women in front of me are turning over their orange ration cards in exchange for bread. It is then, looking over their shoulders, that I notice their cards are stamped for 5.25 ounces, about a half loaf of bread.

I look down again at my card. It clearly says 2 ounces! Anger boils in me again. Over the head of Mr. and Mrs. Zherdev, the Ukrainian bakers, is a crisp new poster of Adolf Hitler. It is pasted over the old, greasy one of Comrade Stalin—you can still see one red corner of his poster peeking out from where the flour paste hadn't held. I glare at Hitler's image.

I take a deep breath when I reach the glass counter, crosshatched with scratches. I hold out my ration card and look Mrs. Zherdev in the eye, anger making me bold. I don't know where his name came from, but it comes to me at that moment: "Mr. Davydenko, who you know is the chief of police, asked me to tell you to give me double this card. He is a client of mine and Mrs. Petrovich."

I see her look at her husband. He squints his small eyes at me in the dimness of the shop, lit only by the sun shining in dusty motes around those horrible large, square Lwów posters that block out most of the light now.

He shrugs and calls up the next customer.

Mrs. Zherdev weighs out 4 ounces and puts the quarter loaf in my basket. I hold my breath till I get out the door, then try to shake out my fury by running, bread bouncing in the basket. I only stop once to relieve myself in the roadside bushes.

I can't say anything when I put down on the table the basket with a larger chunk of bread. Mama takes me in her arms. I just shake and shiver, too angry to cry.

"You are clean, my Hanna, you are beautiful," my mother's singsong voice whispers into my hair, the hair that has gotten us more food to eat.

"You are worthy."

There is still one person I can count on, besides Leon, to treat me the same, as clean and worthy. That is Mrs. Petrovich. In fall, she needs my help more than usual as she starts preparing for the next Easter season.

You see, Mrs. Petrovich is a well-known *pysanka* maker, a descendant of the Hutsuls in the Carpathian Mountains, who believe the world depends on women like her to make many *pysanky* for Easter. No war has ever stopped her. In fact, she makes more during hard times.

The decorated eggs are given away as talismans by Christians at Easter. Even though we don't celebrate Easter, and the second commandment states that we cannot make likenesses of what is in the heavens or what is on the earth, with much reluctance Mama and Papa let me work in our neighbor's kitchen to help fill the many orders she gets from all over the countryside. Mama has to return the favor of having our Sabbath fire lit each week, and a jar of preserves just isn't enough. I am the favor.

Mama's first rule is that I cannot bring any of the eggs into our home, as much as I want to own one. "You must worship the Creator, not creativity," she teaches us. Her second rule is that I cannot discuss the process with my sister and brother.

I know my role well, which is to help Mrs. Petrovich clean the chicken and goose eggs, prepare the dye, wash the eggs when she is done, then rub them with olive oil and varnish them. The special apron she made for me now hangs on a wooden peg by her front door. Over that door, she always hangs a dried bunch of silver-green mugwort leaves to ward off evil witches. I also return her supplies to a cupboard high up in her kitchen, which she can no longer reach, and scrub her table with rock salt when we are through, so she can eat her supper on it later. Before scrubbing I clean off any stray bread crumbs from earlier meals, careful not to let any drop to the floor, because Mama taught me that to let the crumbs fall on the ground might bring poverty into a home.

The table's wood is stained in rainbow colors, like her hands.

On this day, when I arrive after school, she is already melting beeswax over candle flame. I love the smell of her home—a mix of beeswax, melted candle wax, burning wicks, vinegar, and varnish. I inhale when I lift the iron latch and open the wooden door and put down my books. I also love the embroidered *rushnyk* towels that hang over her sepia-colored pictures of saints with haloes over their heads. Once, when I'd paused to study the colorful flowers and scrolly designs sewn onto them, she told me they were meant to protect the home. I thought she meant the saints at first, but she meant the *rushnyks*.

"Ah, Hanna, close the door fast, this is a cold September." The draft through the door blows out her candle, and she strikes a wood match on the rough section of her wall-mounted iron match safe, and gets the candle lit again.

"So how is my assistant today?"

"I am well, Mrs. Petrovich."

I go to the hook next to the door, take down my birthday gift, and wrap the ties around my waist. Having my own apron makes me feel older and important.

She watches me over the wavering candle, a *kistka* in one hand to draw on the wax, and an empty egg in the other to decorate. The only other light in the whitewashed cottage is a kerosene lantern at the edge of the table and one on the kitchen counter by the sink. The light thrown by candle and lamps is honey-colored, and flickers across her lined face. She looks sad to me today, tired. It's as if she has dirt in the lines of her face, her wrinkles are so deep. She wears her faded head scarf even inside.

"Hanna, you are fourteen and have worked for me for a long time." When she looks down, her coral necklaces sway. Dots and circles begin to appear on the smooth oval shell canvas. "My name is Alla. You should call me Alla."

"All right, Mrs. Petrovich—" I break off and laugh. "I mean, Alla."

It is strange to call an adult by her first name. But it also feels good, as if she is letting me into her world more. I am grateful for her loyalty. We have been shut out by so many people in town lately.

"Can you boil some willow tree leaves for me?"

I go out to the blue-painted iron pump on her side of the street, pump the long, curved handle up and down, then carry back a tin bucket of water for the pot on the stove. I throw in handfuls of leaves that will make green dye.

Color means everything on these eggs. Green is for the victory of life over death, and spring or rebirth; brown symbolizes Mother Earth; orange is for strength; yellow is used to symbolize the harvest, or light; and red is my favorite color, as it signifies joy. Who does not want joy in their lives? Black, however, as you might guess, is for death, or eternity. The artist can take black and make it mean something more than you would think. Alla uses dark colors for older clients, as this means their lives have been filled; for their children, she uses a lot of white, because they are basically blank pages.

She teaches me that what she draws into the design has meaning. When clients have a sick relative, she covers the egg in wheat stalks, to bring health. When a client says she has a friend who is feeling down and needs support, she draws horses or oak leaves, for strength.

Alla teaches me about spirits. And that everything in nature means something. That the world outside is basically a map for us, with all the guidance and answers we need. That we just have to learn how to read it.

As the water bubbles and pops to the boiling level, I look over her shoulder. She is laddering the egg vertically. "This is for Mrs. Davydenko. She wants to give this to her husband to ensure prosperity for them."

Mr. Davydenko—the police chief whose name I had just used to get more bread. So now he really is a client. I make a mental note to use his name, and Mrs. Davydenko's, again.

Alla sighs. Leaning back in her chair, she puts the egg into a bowl with yellow dye and covers it with a rag to weigh it down, then rubs her eyes with her knotted hands, freckled with multicolored splotches. "It is getting harder to see my designs. My eyes feel cloudy."

"How many orders do you have this year?"

"Almost more than I can make. People are desperate." When I look at her, confused, she taps the wooden chair beside her, inviting me to sit.

"I have told you what all this means on the surface, but you do not know why I make these, and why we think they are so important in our culture."

Her cloudy eyes are like soft blue flannel blankets, almost dark blue in this light. Again, I sense a sadness I haven't seen before.

"My people were once sun worshippers, long before the man who we believed was Christ was born. In the spring, we made these eggs and gave them away as talismans. Because the sun god was the most important deity in our religion, birds were the sun's chosen creations because they were the only ones, man or beast, who could even come close to him in flight. We humans could not catch birds or be a bird, but we could get to their eggs, a source of life. Hence, the importance of the eggs."

This is something I didn't know, that Alla's people did not always follow Christ, that there was a time even before then. I feel some connection to her now, as eggs are an important symbol in our religion, as well. On the Passover plate we serve a *beitzah*, a roasted egg that also symbolizes life.

"We came to believe that the world depended on these eggs. If we women stop making them, evil in the shape of a serpent chained to a cliff will overrun the world. Every year, the serpent sends out his minions to check on us, to see how many we are making. I think . . ." She pauses. "I think, as do many of my people, that the *führer* is the serpent, and the Wehrmacht are his minions. He has stolen our sun symbol, the broken cross, for his own evil design. He is not worthy of it. That is why I need to make as many as I can this year, my Hanna. I need to protect our people." Her eyes sheen over.

"I need to protect *you*." She lays a damp hand on my knee, pats it, and turns away.

"We leave the eggs whole so they have power, but the egg yolk inside is more precious now than ever. I am breaking with tradition and blowing out the shells to give the yolks to neighbors who can't get meat." She nods to an open fruit jar on the table filled with clear shiny liquid and large sunny yolks and yellow swirls from the ones that had broken when blowing them through the egg holes.

"Let us get back to our important work, which we do in secret to protect the eggs from the evil eye."

She removes the shell from the yellow dye and I dry it for her, so she can draw on the next layer of wax. Soon the egg transforms into a multilayered tiny world of ladders and deer and willow branches dripping down, in yellows and reds, and browns and blacks. *How can such a small, delicate thing save anyone?* I think.

But I do believe that Mrs. Davydenko, who has unwittingly helped my family get more bread, will be very happy to give it to her husband in the spring. And he will be very happy to receive it.

Our time is coming. The SS begin to invade even the smaller rural villages in the countryside in their gray-green uniforms and their dark gray motor coats, on motorbikes and trucks, carrying their terrifyingly efficient brown Mauser rifles. On a beautiful September Sunday, they drive through Kwasova, with ragged lines of exhausted Romanian Jews trailing behind their trucks, trying to keep up on bloody and blue bare feet. Many with no coats, bound for the labor camps and ghettoes up north.

I stand with Symon and Leeba on the hill behind our house, watching the long dark line snake through the northern part of the town road, the paved one that leads to other towns and villages. It stops in the market square, and becomes a large gathering of tiny dark soldiers, looking like ants scurrying around the mound of an anthill. The square looks deserted now. The merchants must have gotten word and locked their doors and pulled their shutters and gone into hiding. Even Poles and peasants do not want to be around when the SS come through.

Shuttered doors and windows mean nothing. Soldiers break down locked doors and smash windows and carry bushels and bags and boxes of what little food they can find back to their trucks. They take a few horses that are still tied to posts, their owners having fled so fast they had been forced to leave them behind. The Germans use horses to pull their war weapons and supplies.

"They are taking what's left of our food," Leeba says quietly.

"I wish I was old enough to fight them!" Symon stamps his feet and crushes the grass around him in frustration.

We stay on the hill for hours, too afraid to go home for a meal, even though our stomachs are complaining. We have to make sure they are not going to backtrack south to our home. They enter the town hall where the Ukrainian police, growing in numbers and wearing discarded German uniforms, have their headquarters and a makeshift prison. The captured Jews huddle together in the square for warmth.

My heart breaks to see their misery. How I wish I had many scarves to hand out. Then, the sounds of distant motors revving up, and the line moves north again, with soldiers on the stolen horses, and the horses whinnying with anxiety as they leave their owners behind. We breathe a collective sigh of relief when they are gone, and then pray that these

Romanians, whom we could not help, will be safe and find food and warmth in the ghettoes.

The Cohan brothers give my parents the shocking news. While staying with a peasant farmer up north in a village near Borszczów, they watched from the hayloft of his barn as our group of Romanian prisoners was driven into a deep river.

"These Jews, they did not know how to swim. They either drowned or were shot by the soldiers in the back if they made it to the other side," Pavel says, banging what must have been his fist up and down on the kitchen table. "Women and children, too!"

"The soldiers played music while they watched," Jacob says quietly. "It was not of this world. The gramophone sending such beautiful classical notes through the valley while this slaughter took place. The music could not cover the sounds of the drowning or the machine gun fire."

I am listening at the top of the stairs again. I feel sick to my stomach. Scared. War is coming closer. People I have seen, who walked on our roads, are being murdered. Proof that Jews are being lied to. There are no safe camps or ghettoes any longer. Blood pounds in my ears. My head hurts. I go back to my soft goose down mattress and comforter and try not to think of what I just heard, to erase it somehow. I say the Shema, and after many feverish hours of tossing and turning, I fall into an exhausted sleep. I dream of guns firing and water splashing.

The next morning, Papa and Mama come into our bedroom, and Papa tells us we are not to go to school for a while. I knew that day was coming, but now it is here.

"The SS issued orders to the Ukrainian police and the Jewish Council. Jews are now being ordered to register and to make their own armbands, a blue Mogen Dovid, our Jewish star, sewn on to a white background. I won't let my family be branded in this way. It is a dangerous beginning. We must all stay home these next few days of registration."

Symon asks from his bed, looking very worried, "But will someone tell them about us?"

"Though it's an offense to hide Jews, I'm counting on our neighbors not turning us in. They are not actively hiding us, just keeping quiet, forgetting who we are." He glances over at Mama and nods his head, as if to reassure her, too.

Papa is still too essential to their daily lives. But he knows, as Mama and I do from our experiences getting bread, that his standing in Kwasova is at risk. I see in my mind again those posters in the window, the big red letters, the lice, the blaming of Jews for the war.

Someday, someone will betray us. For money, for food, for their own lives spared.

My parents' focus must now shift from helping those who are escaping to helping ourselves. The barn, where the Romanians used to hide, is no longer a safe place. The Cohans tell us the SS, and the Ukrainian police, who now are turning in Jews, are learning that barns are the main place to look for them—under dusty hay and worm-holed floorboards. They also tell us that the SS have long been surrounding towns and villages and herding Jews into the market squares and forcing them to march to ghettoes or are murdering them in plain sight. Without radios and telephones for the general population, months of atrocities have taken place without our knowledge. Even the Cohans have only heard small bits. Ukrainian neighbors have gone silent.

Uncle Levi helps Papa and some other Jewish neighbors dig underground bunkers at night, among bushes shading the edges of the wheat fields and sheep meadows, where we used to hold Sukkōt. Those bunkers would be for the men and older boys. They could run faster than the women and girls and deal with harsher conditions. The bunkers, lined with damp logs, have air vents hidden in brush above.

For the women, they build attic bunkers, sealing off the sides under pitched roofs to make fake walls. Our bunker door is at the foot of my bed and Leeba's. She and I are taught to make sure all the beds in the house are made up every morning, so as not to look like someone is living in the house and had hastily left, and to make sure nothing is out of place. Messy makes it obvious someone is in hiding. Dishes are washed immediately after eating, dried, and put away.

We decide to sleep in our clothes at night, so we aren't caught in our sleepwear without warning.

When we can get a bit of flour from trading with Ivan Umański, we bake small biscuits at night so the smoke is not visible and the kitchen is also clean when the targeted invasions, or *Aktions* as some are now calling them, take place. We hear hushed whispers that the Gestapo, the German secret police who are beginning to replace the Einsatzgrüppen, will soon come to Kwasova.

An axe and some steel rods stand by the front and back doors, along with a bucket of sand to throw in the faces of any invaders if they force themselves in. Even children can throw sand, and Papa tells us we should fight if necessary. Hitler has issued a "Regulation Against Jews' Possession of Weapons." Anyone found with a weapon is shot on sight. Even though Papa has not owned a gun before, we still have to defend ourselves with something Papa can approve of and keep in sight without calling suspicion on himself.

Papa reluctantly removes the metal *mezuzah* from the doorpost and fills in the holes and paints it over, so there is no evidence that it has hung there for years, protecting us and the tiny religious Hebrew scroll within. He places it carefully in a cloth bag, for safekeeping. He tells Mama he is not ready to have it buried in the Jewish cemetery, where *mezuzahs* are taken when an owner passes and the house no longer houses someone of the Jewish faith. "We will return to hang it again."

"The Gestapo and the SS are known to come mainly in the daylight," the Cohan brothers tell us. "They do not want to chase Jews and peasants in the dark. We know our way around too well, know where the streams and fox holes and large stones are that could trip up a German soldier."

Still, Papa removes a pane of glass from the small window by my bed with a knife, and each of us takes turns listening in the dark for early warning sounds of artillery shooting or boots marching or tanks rolling.

One quiet night, I lie in bed, tossing and turning, worrying, not able to sleep, watching the cold moonlight etch Papa's face with the crosses of wood that surround and hold the glass panes. His face looks like it is behind bars. He sees my open eyes, and slides over to my side and strokes my head. "Remind me to teach you children about the first line of the Shema tomorrow night."

He keeps stroking till my scalp relaxes, then my mind, then my body, and I sleep, lulled by the comfort of a strong, loving father.

"Shema Yisrael, Adonai Eloheinu, Adonai echad. Hear, O Israel, the Lord is our God, the Lord is One."

We lie on our beds and repeat our nightly prayer, our eyes closed, covering them with our right hands, as we had been taught to do since we were old enough to speak the words. Symon is still memorizing it.

"Blessed be the Name of the glory of His glorious kingdom forever and ever."

Papa sits with us, watching, not joining in tonight. He explains for the first time, "You say this before you go to bed each night. You cover your eyes so there is no distraction. You say the second part quietly because we are not fit to bless God. This night-prayer helps keep away the demons. And you say this every night, children, but the first line is special. You must say the first line when . . . when . . ."

He doesn't—can't—finish.

We wait for him, the seconds ticking by like thunderclaps.

He rises and quietly leaves.

Later, when we are underground, I will learn what he wanted to say, but couldn't, at that moment.

Tonight it is Mama's night to listen at the window. Leeba, Symon, and I fall asleep to the murmurings of the prayer, which tonight we repeat over and over till we lose consciousness.

"Wake up!"

Mama is shaking the whole bed.

I come to, out of a deep well of sleep. It takes some time to make sense of what she is saying.

"Into the bunkers! Make the bed—fast!"

Symon is already up and has his bed made. Leeba and I jump out of bed, not questioning, just doing what we've been taught to do so many times before.

Papa and Symon slip down the stairs and out the back door.

I can now hear what sounds like heavy boots approaching the house from down the lane, grinding the dirt and gravel with their murderous purpose.

Mama pulls back the hidden door, and we slip into a crouching position, sitting one in front of the other, as if on a sled. She pulls the door closed.

We forgot the chamber pot! I scream inside my head. I try to remember if any of us had used it. It is too late to get it.

Banging on the front door and cries of "*Alle Juden heraus!* All Jews out!"

The crash of bayonets breaking the locked latch on the door, the sound of fast footsteps on the first floor. Heavy military boots. Big tall SS boots.

A mouse skitters over my feet and I squeal. Mama's hard knuckles hit the back of my head hard. I see little stars in the dark.

Footsteps up the stairs. A lump in my throat. I cover my mouth with my blanket in case another mouse runs by.

Footsteps into my parents' small room, then into ours. Circling like lions.

A few light raps on the walls. In our inner space, they are explosions, one near my right ear, but because we are stuffed in, the space doesn't sound hollow.

More German words, then the footsteps retreat.

My stomach hurts. I whimper inside.

It is hard to stay in the crawlspace, trying not to make a sound, bent over, dozing off here and there while sitting up, wrapped in blankets we had stored in the spaces. When we can't hold it in any longer, Mama tells us to pee into the blankets.

It goes against instinct to relieve yourself in your own clothes. But we have no choice. I force myself to relax, till I feel a warm flow. It feels shameful.

Papa knocks on our wall two days later, telling us all is clear. We crawl out, stiff and bleary-eyed, our clothes wet and soiled, parched for water, hungry for food.

Mama reaches for me and hugs me hard. She has never hit any of us.

"I am so sorry, Hanna. But we can make no noise at all. I will hit you again if I have to. Know it is because I am trying to keep you alive."

I bury my head into her shoulder when she says that, tired of the fear we are now constantly living under. I feel sick and dizzy.

Little did I know—there would be harder times.

We are allowed back to school for a few quiet days, our parents and teachers trying to keep our lives as normal as possible. But those days are happening less and less. We shift in our seats, fidget, fail tests, stare out windows, and jump when the recess bell is rung. Teachers are talking of closing the school altogether or moving the school to the basement of the Polish Community Center, to hold secret classes.

At lunchtime, we sit around eating our small meals. We can now only get food off our own land or by trading with Ukrainians in the *shtetele* or with peasants in the valley. Some Poles who remain, like the flour miller, have known Papa for years and quietly continue to trade with him, even though it is now against the law. Papa's skills at mending things keep us somewhat fed, as he trades his skills now for food rather than silver *kopecks* or paper *złotych*.

Mama's garden of potatoes, sugar beets, carrots, and beans and her fruit trees also feed us. It has been a long time since we have been able to get kosher meat, or any meat, for our usual meals of *cholent* and smoked sausage and stuffed cabbage. We are down to breads and cheeses and root vegetables, fruits and berries. Auntie Maya's family has started eating what little meat they are able to buy that is not kosher, using up their money and jewelry to buy it from anyone who will sell to them, but Papa will not yet give in.

On the last school afternoon in 1942, near the Yom Kippur holiday, before the Germans force the Ukrainian police in our *shtetele* to shut down the schools to all children for good, I read from *Joan of Arc,* copy out a quotation that I like, and pick at some dry bread. We had recently traded wool for flour. That was two weeks ago, and now the flour barrel is empty.

Yesterday, when we got home from school, we found all the sheep gone. The Ukrainian police had taken the herd to feed the SS, in return for keeping quiet about our family, who still do not wear armbands. Now there is no more wool to trade. Ovid looks bewildered every day, pacing around the sheep pens, nose to the ground, and Symon sniffles. The sheep were gentle friends to him.

Leon sits next to me. Normally this would make me quiver, but today I am too depressed to register his heat and his presence. It turns out I am not as depressed as Leon, however.

"I turned sixteen today," he says. "And no one noticed. . . ."

I look at his profile. He is focusing down, at his feet, his hands shoved in a jacket that probably fit him well a year ago, when he had turned fifteen. I am so lost in my own misery, I didn't notice he had no lunch. I can't offer him my stale bread, the edges soggy with saliva where I'd gnawed it, but I have a handful of dried crabapples in my bag.

"For your birthday," I say, feeling shy about it, holding out all the shriveled fruit to him in my cupped hand.

He looks down, then up at me, and I see a small smile tweak the corners of his lips just a little. His green eyes always alarm me in a good way, and even now, his dimple makes me want to touch his face, to put my finger in the little dent. When he takes the apples, opening his connected palms so I can fill them like a bowl, I brush his curled fingers. The hairs stand out on the back of my neck. It feels like a small, innocent electrical volt. He chews each crabapple slowly, looking out beyond the fence to the market square on the other side. The market is mostly empty.

He says, between bites, "I'm tired of hiding in our neighbor's wall when the *Aktions* come. You are lucky the soldiers don't come as far out as your place so often. They took away the Weinsteins last week. But . . . we are still free. I hear the camps are terrible places. And many Jews are not making it to the camps, digging their own trenches to die in."

This is another rumor we have recently heard, but it is

easy to put it away at the back of our minds as hearsay. So when Leon repeats it, the rumor sounds real to me for the first time. But he would know, because his father is friendly with the police chief, Mr. Davydenko.

"I wonder if I will see seventeen."

"Don't say that!" I yell. I feel my face flush with anger, and I stand up. "We are all going to survive, I just know we are, and you are *not* going to say that again!" I point a furious finger at him.

He stares at me, startled. Then, to my surprise, he laughs.

And laughs, till he wipes tears from his eyes. "Oh, Hanna, my spunky friend Hanna, you will keep us all alive, won't you? If a German soldier saw you right now, he would run."

And then the other children around us are laughing, too, caught up with the sound they rarely hear anymore. They begin pointing and shooting at each other. It is child's play; it is how the younger children cope. Poles against Ukrainians. Jews against Poles.

Leon and I sit close to each other. I can feel the energy from his threadbare jacket reach my side, and it is the most comfort I have received in weeks. His breath whispers against my ear when he turns toward me.

This is the best part of being alive, I think. We watch the war games in silence, sharing our sadness. Some Jewish families have fled west, some have been caught by the Germans during the *Aktions* and taken to the Borszczów ghetto or to the German police farm in Skala.

Avrum, the most aggressive Jewish boy of the group, takes prisoners till the teacher calls us back in for the last time.

Kicking road stones on the way home from visiting our cousins, I try to kick them farther than Leeba and Symon. We ignore the same bullies who still like to follow us and call us names.

"Communists!" they now shout. The Germans are trying everything to turn our neighbors against us. Now they are telling Ukrainians and Poles that Jews are communists, plotting against them, and that we sacrifice babies and eat them.

Symon uses his sling shot again, hits two of them, and they scatter. When we make it to our door without further trouble, I leave my brother and sister and walk across the street to Alla's. Her home, like many of the Hutsuls' homes, has one front door and one window set into the right side of the house. On the left is a wall, not broken up by any windows. This is the small barn where she keeps her fowl and two goats. That way she doesn't have to go into snowstorms to feed them, and the wall that the two sides share has a fireplace to keep the animals warm.

She still has the nanny goat, which continues to give her milk because she stimulates it by milking it twice a day. The Ukrainian police took the younger buck but left the older doe with her, because the doe was too old to eat. They also took most of the geese and hens, but left her with her best layers, at the order of Chief Davydenko. His wife relies that much on her *pysanky*.

It is hard for Alla to move fast. Her knees are old, but I hear movement. She opens her blue, flaking door after a few minutes.

"Hanna, what a nice surprise! Come in."

I've seen her home so many times, but today, I wander around as if it is all new. I take in the wood platform bed piled so high with down pillows filled with feathers from her geese that I wonder how she can sleep. I take in the wood racks that hold darkened copper plates and bright blue enamel plates. I take in the *rushnyks*. I take in the forbidden icons.

I am looking for something. But what is it?

My eyes fall on a picture of her and her husband on their wedding day in a carved wood frame. The photo is brown and fuzzy, but you can make out the man's strong nose under a felt hat, and her happy, crinkled eyes under an embroidered scarf. She looks so smooth and young, the shape of her face so different than it is now—round and fallen a bit, but still soft and rosy.

"How did you know he was the one to marry?" I ask. "Did you have a matchmaker?"

"No, I did not."

I feel Alla's gaze pierce me, and I blush.

"He carved his way into my heart," she continues, moving her stiff legs to a hand-carved maple chest at the end of the bed, painted with bright colors. She lifts the top and takes out a Bible, and opens it to another photo, pressed between two pages.

"See this?"

It is the image of a cemetery plot, with a casket next to open ground. The casket is the most beautiful wooden box I've ever seen. Carved with stars and flowers and birds that swirl together.

"He did this for my mother, before we were courting," is all she says, gently caressing the photo.

"When we bury the dead in our Jewish cemetery," I tell her, "we use plain pine boxes or nothing at all, just a shroud."

"I know. It is a wonderful way to make sure everyone is treated equally and honors the belief that we all return to the earth." She pats me on my arm. "I believe every culture has something to offer. Your way may be better."

She places the photo back between the pages, seems to hesitate. "He still eats with me on Christmas Eve." She says this to me softly, as if she is afraid of what I might think.

I had seen an extra spot at her table on her past holiday, but had not wanted to ask. Alla lives so close to the earth and spirits, I am not surprised to find out that this is how she dines sometimes.

"When he died," she says, "I did not leave his shirt open, which would have allowed me to marry again. I buttoned it tightly to the top.

"Come here," she says, "let me do something for you. It should be done in November on the eve of one of my holidays, St. Andrew's Day, yes? But nothing is as it should be lately, so why should we follow the rules ourselves?"

She walks slowly to her wood rack and, from the shelf above, takes down a blue enamel bowl with a black line around the rim. It has rust spots on it, as does most of our own enamelware. She fills it with well water from the bucket in the sink. "The wax is in a drawer over there. Let's melt it."

She takes a wood match and strikes it against the match safe near the stove, then holds the flame to the end of the wax and lets the drippings fall on the water's surface. Instantly the wax hardens into blobs and swirls. I watch, fascinated and excited.

"All right, it's done."

She blows out the match, puts the wax stick on a plate, takes a wood spoon from a crock, and lifts the wax image.

"Take it to the window and hold it to the light."

There is only the one window at the front of the cottage. I hold up the warm wax to the setting sun. The wax turns orangey.

She looks over my shoulder. "Your future is in there. Look for something, anything you recognize. A shape, a tool, an object. It will tell you what trade your husband-to-be is in."

I jump when she says the word *husband*. Is that what I was searching for?

The wax had swirled into curls at the top, then left lacy openings in the center. I can see my home through it. At the bottom are several thick blobs. Try as I can, I can't see anything that resembles a shape or occupation that might be related to Leon, or any other young man from the *shtetele*. I sigh.

"Nothing? Then pay attention tonight to your dreams."

She tells me to keep the wax prophecy.

I take it home, hiding it under my sweater so Mama won't see. When I go upstairs, it is already broken. I look at the waxy mess, then throw it out the upstairs bedroom window into the yard. Who am I to dream of a future?

Everything is coming to pieces. I cannot see beyond the next hour, something that is starting to weigh heavily on me, on all of us.

That night it's my turn to listen at our window, my ear to the open square space where the glass pane used to be. The cool fall breezes push into my ear, as Leon's breath had. I think about what Leon said. Would *I* live to be fifteen? I had acted so sure of myself, but deep down, I wonder. I wonder why God would make one set of people who want to destroy another. Papa says to keep faith, but my faith is in him and my family.

The night is blessedly quiet, and despite pinching my arm several times near dawn to keep awake, I doze off to the sounds of my brother and sister turning in the sheets, and the soft sounds of wild nocturnal animals rustling about the barn.

Soon, I am rocking back and forth in a dream. Something feathery, something white and gentle brushes over my head. Rocking. My head is cool, but my feet burn in a tub of boiling wax.

The most holy day of the year, the Day of Atonement, or Yom Kippur, approaches, and we prepare secretly. We remove our leather boots, because we cannot ask for God's forgiveness while wearing the skin of a slaughtered animal. We fast (Symon and Leeba are too young, so are allowed some bread and water), to make our bodies uncomfortable and make us aware of other people's discomfort, though being hungry these days is becoming a habit. We pray and ask for forgiveness.

But this is not a year to gather in the synagogue for services. In fact, the synagogue, with its beautiful sky-blue ceiling decorated with silver Mogen Dovids, is now the headquarters of the Judenrat, the Jewish Council, hired to watch over their own people (Papa refused the offer to join). Rabbi Rosenthal has disappeared. The Jewish families who are left quietly worship at home now, even on the Sabbath.

SEPTEMBER 26, 1942, FIRST EVENING OF SUKKŌT—

Five days after Yom Kippur, we are all gathered around the table, gently repeating the HaMotzi, the prayer made over a small piece of *challah*. *"Baruch atah Adonai, Eloheinu Melech haolam—"*

A rapid knock on the back door echoes loudly through the kitchen.

We look at each other in fear. No one ever knocks on the back door. Papa picks up an axe and opens it slowly.

Alla stands on the stone stoop, the face beneath her flowered kerchief bright red in the light that falls on it from the open door, and her brow is furrowed; she holds a wooden cross in each hand.

"Abram." She enters quickly. "I know you will not like to do this, but you *must*. For the children," she says urgently, looking at all of us looking at her, our mouths open in surprise.

"I took eggs to the Davydenko's today, and they said that tonight, Kwasova will be the focus of a German invasion. A Gestapo chief, named Koelner, is coming through here, on his way to meet with Hitler. He has declared the town be *Judenfrei*, free of *all* Jews. Christians are to put a cross on their front doors as a private signal to the Gestapo and the SS that there are no Jews to be found in the house. I know this is an insult on the eve of your holiday, and that is why they are coming tonight, hoping you will be distracted. You must put this on your door. And here is another cross for Eva's sister. I only have two spare ones, or I would give more."

Poor Papa. He stands in his stockings, staring at the out held crosses. How much of his life has been about upholding our beliefs, and now, to save us, he has to take the holiest of Christian symbols that is being used to destroy us and put it on his home.

I cross my arms and shiver from the sharp cold coming through the door. Soon, it will be dark. Black. And who knows what is coming with that blackness.

"Abram?" Mama calls to him softly.

He lowers his face for a moment, then puts down the axe and holds out his hands. Alla gives him the crosses.

I rush over and hug Alla, who hugs me back. Alla is helping us again.

"I have to take this to Levi right now. I'll be back as soon as I can." Papa puts the crosses on the kitchen table and sits down on a bench to put his boots on. "Symon, get one of those crosses on the door *now*. The hammer is hanging in the broom closet."

Symon steps forward and hesitates. One cross is simple, just two highly polished branches nailed together. The other one looks as if Alla had decorated it—intricate carvings mimicking her *pysanky* patterns, filled with color enamel and embellishing the full surface. I wonder if her husband carved it. Symon picks that one and runs for the closet. Soon, he is standing on a stool and hammering the cross onto our front door, while Papa gallops off on Steed, the only horse we have left, to deliver the other cross to our cousins.

We wait around the kitchen table for him to return, pretending to do small tasks.

He comes back quickly, bolts the doors, closes the curtains so there is no crack between them, then sits down with us.

The candle burns and flickers in the center of the oiled wooden boards, sending shadows that look alive against the walls and cloth window hangings. He sings briefly in prayer. I can't concentrate on the beautiful chants. Papa's deep voice tonight sounds ragged. On a night that is supposed to be joyous and thankful, we are about to be invaded.

No time for the rest of the ceremony, we spend Sukkōt hiding everything we inherited or own that is religious or valuable. We had heard that the Germans were taking what they could, some as bribes for promises of no *Aktion*, so we save a few things in case we need them, but hide under our beds our beautiful, intricate silver menorah and our heavy silver Sabbath candlesticks, along with Papa's family jewelry, a watch, silver spoons, and Mama's Kiddush cup. After the invasion, if the cross works and we can go out again, we will transfer the valuables to the sheep shacks and outhouse, digging them into the corners of the dirt floors, where the Germans are less likely to look than in the barn.

On the chance that the Germans might knock on the door even if they see a cross, we all have to hide.

I know to make no sound this time. The air is stale and dusty. My breath is hot and shallow. We'd remembered this time to leave a bucket in the bunker for relieving ourselves.

Time ticks by. There is no clock in here, but I can hear it ticking away.

Tick... Tick...

Second by second. Minute by minute.

Tick... Tick...

But no knock comes.

The next morning, Papa knocks on our wall and says it is safe to come out. We crawl back into the unknown.

We are still afraid to leave the house. We listen at the window.

Then hear a horse galloping down the road.

It is Stepan Illiouk, whose farm fields are north of the abandoned schools. His eyes are wild and he speaks in quick bursts.

"Your cousins are safe. The invasion is over."

We all breathe a sigh of relief and cling to each other in joy.

He holds up his hands to stop us from being too happy.

He tells us that Koelner's men had passed by our home

and circled the town and chased down many of the remaining Jews. The Judenrat tried to pay them off, as they had paid other SS soldiers off in the past, but Koelner would not hear of it. He even arrested some of the councilmen. Then the raid began of the homes that had no crosses on them. They pillaged what they could find and rounded up in the market square those who were able to walk. They shot the ones in bed who could not move. Then they took a few healthy ones from the square and put them in trucks, bound for the Janowska camp, and the rest were herded to the farmer's fields, to a natural culvert. They were lined up, a few at a time, and shot so they fell in. All during this nightmarish time, all through the night, the Germans played music and ate stolen food. Bach and Mozart wafted over his threshed fields, almost masking the sounds of gunshot. . . . They ordered the Ukrainian police to cover over the bodies, even while some bodies still moved.

He weeps, in that way that an older man can weep, trying to hold it in but unable. Small sobs burst out, as he tries to gulp them down.

"I now . . . have a graveyard . . . on the edge of my grain field."

We weep with him, holding each other. It is hard to take in. I think of Esther in the Bible, and how she was able to save her people. How could I not do so? I think of Joan, and all the warring and death that surrounded her. How had she survived it? This isn't the time of the ancient Achaemenid Empire or the Middle Ages, but it feels just as dangerous. We now realize this is not a shorter-lived, isolated outbreak of violence against Jews, a pogrom as Papa calls it. This is annihilation.

And what of Leon? I'm frantic and exhausted with worry about him. Mr. Illiouk had hidden the Cohan brothers behind his living room wall, so we know they are safe.

Papa asks Mr. Illiouk if he can get us word about the Stadnicks.

I walk around in a daze, doing nothing, until Mr. Illiouk comes back to the house that evening with a small sack of supplies as an excuse to visit, with terror still in his eyes. We learn that the Stadnicks survived due to their wealth (they paid a Polish neighbor most of their savings so he would hide them). Marc and Sonia Rabinowitz, friends of my aunt and uncle, survived in Mr. Umański's mill, under dusty white flour sacks he'd draped over them.

Mr. Illiouk warns us that even some of our past sympathizers are changing. Fedir Woliński, the Polish lamplighter and Symon's old friend, was named a *Tzeler,* a Counter. He will now patrol for the Germans, the SS whom Koelner left behind to further organize and expand the Ukrainian police to now include disbanded German militiamen, conscripted young Ukrainians, and foreign mercenaries. Like before, the lamplighter will patrol at night. He will look for Jews in hiding and keep records of the dead in the *shtetele* and surrounding valley for the invaders, who want to see large numbers and keep track of who is still evading capture.

Chief Davydenko is now to turn in *all* Jews, but for those few on the Jewish Council who had been let go during the *Aktion,* but now even these Judenrat are being asked to turn in their own.

Avrum, the little boy at school who had fought in the war game that fall day, was chased down this afternoon by a council member, turned in, and sent away to a work camp. Or so we hoped. Many rivers and fields and town centers we now know have become final resting places. Papa moans in private sorrow that there was no Kaddish, no mourner's prayer, to honor the departed.

Mr. Illiouk unloads his sack in the barn, and in return Symon and Papa hand him up a sack of potato spuds for the next planting season, some dried apples, and a goose. Leeba holds the goose one last time, tears streaming down her red cheeks. The goose struggles and squawks till they cover its head.

Leeba says, "Good-bye, goose," and runs inside.

"I can't come here again," the kind farmer says sadly. "They are taking those of us who help, too. I think you must leave Kwasova as soon as possible. The cross won't help for long. Someone will turn you in. Look what happened to Avrum. Everyone is hungry now and a hungry man will do anything not to see his family starve. Go see Yuri. He maybe can help you find a place to hide. He knows the forest like the back of his hand."

"I know, Stepan. I know you cannot help anymore. And my family and I much appreciate what you have done for us. God will remember you."

"And you and your family, Abram. God be with you. We pray to God differently, no? But I think we pray for the same things."

And with that, he sits straight up on his bench, snaps the reins in the cool air, whistles, and the wagon rolls away over the rutted road.

I will never see him again.

Back inside, as soon as he closes the door, Papa turns to Mama. "Stepan says it is time to go."

She is at the sink, peeling potatoes with a knife. The peels become thicker and the skinned white potatoes, smaller, for the minute she is silent. Then she stops, wrists resting on the front lip of the soapstone sink, and looks up. I hadn't noticed before a gray streak on the right side of her hair.

"It is something we know how to do well, leave a place. So be it."

OCTOBER 1942–

First, the geese are slaughtered and their downy feathers plucked and boiled and dried for quilts and pillows. I sit nights at the kitchen table with Mama and Leeba, peeling the fluffy part of the feather from the quills. The fluff gets stuffed into cotton pillowcases and scrap quilts. Leeba sniffles the whole time, sad at the loss of her flock. Papa uses the poultry meat to trade for kerosene and matches. Mama saves one goose carcass to make soup. Papa is giving in about meat being kosher. He knows we need meat.

We pack all our clothes into bundles. I fold my one good dress with the daisy pattern that Mama had sewn (I do not know if I will wear it in the forest but I can't leave it behind), a long-sleeve school blouse and long skirt (I am wearing the other set), two sets of darned knee socks, one pair of wool tights, one slip, one nightgown, one wool sweater, and two pair of underwear.

"Leave behind your good shoes," Mama directs. "Just bring your leather boots."

Leeba has been trying to stuff into her bundle her shiny black leather shoes. They close with a strap held by a round white shell button that looks like a pearl. She is very proud of them. Uncle Levi made them for her for her last birthday.

She sits on the bed and puts her head in her hands and cries.

"I don't want to leave. I don't want to leave my house. I don't want to leave my bed and my school. I don't want to leave my *shoes.*"

Symon and I look on, both feeling awkward. While we would also miss our home, we know it is time to go. It is not "home" anymore. Home is where you are safe. He and I can't wait to get to a safer place.

Mama kneels by Leeba and puts her arm around her. "Leeba, we can replace shoes, we can replace a house, a bed. We can never replace the wonder that is Leeba. We have to go, to save Leeba. And to save Hanna and Symon. Your body is holy and we must protect it. For that is where your spirit lives. To protect Leeba, we have to start thinking more of the spirit than the body. What do you love that is not an object that you can bring?"

Leeba sits quietly. "Umm, maybe . . . my brother and sister?" Mama nods encouragement. "My . . . ability to sew?"

"Yes, Leeba, keep thinking like this and I promise you will not much miss the other things. I have to leave my favorite dress behind, too. I know it is hard."

The giving up continues. Papa gives Steed, our gentle horse, to the miller, and our cow to a sympathetic peasant farmer in the valley. In return, Papa receives flour, more kerosene, cabbages, onions, cheese, and beets. Mama and I mend every piece of clothing that is ripped or needs to be let out. Symon is growing fast and she is worried he will outgrow his pants before we have time to make more. She takes an extra pair of Papa's he'd hidden in his workshop when the Russians confiscated furs and clothing, and she cuts them down for the future.

Papa hides the synagogue's Torah in a new place. Rabbi Rosenthal had taken the parchment scroll, on which the biblical law was inscribed, from the *aron hakodesh*, the Holy Ark where it was stored. The rabbi gave it to the man he most trusted would be able to keep it safe, my father, before our rabbi disappeared and before the old stone building was overrun. The sacred scrolls, wrapped in a purple velvet sash with silken blue Mogen Dovids sewn on, and with their silver engraved page pointer for reading, had been kept in the attic bunker in a special wood box. Now Papa has hidden them in a place that is so secret even we, his family, do not know where they are.

Mama, Leeba, and I pickle and jar whatever is ripe, including the winter pears that are still somewhat green. The barn fills with sacks and boxes of provisions.

It is a bitter harvest.

Symon buries the valuables in several sheep sheds and in the outhouse and keeps a few items for barter. We hear that the last of the Kwasovian Jews, not just the Stadnicks, are bartering food, farm animals, pocket watches, coins, and wedding bands for their lives. Many fingers now are bare.

We are each allowed to keep one thing we value most.

Leeba keeps her sewing kit, and Symon keeps his sling shot. I am at the end of the first chapter in *Joan of Arc*, where Joan, at seventeen, is looking back on her distant village, "trying to print these scenes on her memory." I am doing the same. I keep my birthday book and, tucked into it, the piece of notepaper I have started copying quotations on. Papa needed my full school notebook to trade for food, because paper has become so scarce that it is very valuable now. The only paper I have left is this one piece that I ripped from the notebook before giving it up.

But where are we to go? Where can we hide so that those carrying the flag with the crooked cross will not find us?

Papa disappears for two days. I ask nervously, looking at his empty spot at suppertime on the second night, "Where is he?"

"Not to worry, Hanna, he is finding us a hiding spot."

But I do worry, and I listen that cloudless, long night at the window for his footsteps. I want him home. But the night is too quiet. No sheep even to make their usual reassuring noises.

The harvest moon floats like an enormous drop of amber honey in the inky sky, and I wonder what it is thinking of those tiny little specs running and chasing each other around on the planet below. I suspect the moon, if it could, would step on us like we step on annoying anthills in the schoolyard and in the dirt lanes.

When the moon moves out of sight behind the western tree line, and the dark lifts a bit from the horizon, I crawl into bed and say the Shema. Then I wake to Leeba shaking me.

"Wake up! Papa is home!"

I grab a shawl and run downstairs to find Papa with Mr. Stadnick and the Cohan brothers gathered around the table, talking. Mama is pouring a raw and bitter homemade apple wine for them. We have no more tea or coffee or Kiddush prayer wine.

"It's settled, then," Mr. Stadnick says. "Thank you for helping us."

"The cabins can only fit so many," Papa explains. "I suggest you bunk up with the Rabinowitzes. I paid Chief Davydenko to make sure you two"—he nods at the Cohan brothers—"get special papers to collect metal for the war effort. You will be allowed to come and go with badges that give you special work status. The papers say that you are 'Jews important to the German administration.' Carry them always. You will use the metal wagon to transport goods under cover. You should both be safe, and can get us food when we run out."

The brothers nod their heads in unison.

When the others leave, we sit down to breakfast and Papa explains. "I went to see our local forester and gamekeeper, Yuri Jaṅowski. He is a friend. I have known him for many years while I herded my sheep through his copses. He is highly respected and I trust him. More to the point, he is willing to let us stay in two run-down cabins he no longer uses in the backwoods. They are far enough in that we should be safe for the winter. So far the Germans are hesitant to search the forest for fear of running into Soviet or Ukrainian partisan resistance fighters." He looks up at my mother at this point, and she gives him a half-hearted smile.

"It will be a tight squeeze with your sister's family, but we have no choice. . . ." He looks back down. "Let us pray for Yuri and his continued friendship."

We pray for Yuri, then we pray for our safety and the safety of all Jews and friends to Jews, then we pray for strength to get through the winter. I am not much in the mood to be thanking God for things that seem frightening, like living in the forest, but when we thank God for the food we can finally eat, I join in.

I dig into the *sirniki*, Mama's delicious cheese pancakes that are fried and crispy and hot off the griddle. They are delicious even without the cold sour cream on top that she used to make herself. I wonder when I will have such a delicious meal again. This last one comes at a steep price, as flour is so hard to get, even from the miller. Mama had to use up some of our precious stores and trade a few apples for a bit of farmer's cheese to go in the batter. But she said she wanted to make one last civilized meal on her own stove.

Cooking is difficult not just because we have trouble getting food but because we can no longer get coal. We are forced to use wood for the stove, which is dangerous. You can be shot if you are found gathering it in the woods. We are lucky we have a few old trees on our property. Their gnarled, dry limbs are barely keeping us warm and only supplying us with hot meals now and then.

That afternoon, Symon is told to give the dog, Ovid, to Alla for safekeeping. I go with him. This will be hard. Ovid is not an object to leave behind. While Symon cries into Ovid's long dark fur, and the dog whimpers, I look away and take in the potbellied stove, the worn table with its dyes and tools, the two aprons hanging by the door, the saints' pictures hooded by the *rushnyks*.

I wonder how difficult it will be for her to make her eggs without me around to help get ingredients and bring supplies down from cupboards.

"Thank you for your dog, Symon. He will help me keep death away. Dogs see the old woman in white with the scythe coming and bark and warn their owners."

Then Alla looks at me. "Don't fear the forest, Hanna. Remember the things I have taught you."

I do not want to say good-bye to Alla. So I don't. When her rainbow-colored hands reach for me, I turn and leave the boy and the dog and my friend, just like it is any other day. Alla is not an object, either.

I can't see the dirt road. It is too blurry.

I have one more thing I need to do before I leave our home. I tear a bit off the bottom of the page I had saved from my school notebook. On it I write:

Abram Slivka (my Papa)
Eva Slivka (my Mama)
Hanna Slivka (14 years old, loves to read)
Leeba Slivka (12 years old, loves to sew)
Symon Slivka (10 years old, a really good boy who loves his dog)
Ovid (our dog)
Steed (our horse)
We all lived in this house until October 22, 1942. If you find this, say these names out loud, please, and bury this paper in the yard.

I fold the paper and put it into a tin can that once had herring in it. (I can smell the salty oil left behind, even after being washed, and it makes my stomach growl.) It still has the lid attached on one end. I fold the curled lid back down and tie it closed with string. Then crawl into the bunker space and slide the can into the far corner. It disappears into the darkness, with all the spider webs and dust. No one will be here to make noise anymore when the mice run over it.

We leave on the first cloudy night, so the moon won't betray our fleeing figures.

The Forest

OCTOBER 1942—APRIL 1943

I was afraid, and went deeper into the wood. Then I carved a mark in the bark of a tree, saying to myself, it may be that I am dreaming and have not seen this vision at all. I will come again, when I know that I am awake and not dreaming, and see if this mark is still here; then I shall know.

—COPIED BY HANNA SLIVKA FROM
"IN DOMREMY," CHAPTER VI

IT IS A GOOD THING for us that it is October and there is no snow on the ground to show our footsteps. It is an especially cold harvesttime, and the wind blows strong and hard across the steppe-land meadows and fields we cross. It pierces my *kurtka*, wool hat, and stockings. I miss my scarf.

We climb icy rock walls and push through hedgerows.

Before we step into the forest, I look back over the meadows to the small dark shape that was our home for so many years. From somewhere in the wide valley, a dog barks three times.

"I wonder if that is Ovid saying good-bye," Symon says from behind me.

"I think it is," I respond gently.

"Keep moving, Hanna," Uncle Levi orders, urgency in his voice. He is bringing up the rear, while Papa leads us in the front. We are to break into four groups if anyone starts to follow. But all is quiet, except for the clumps of underbrush that scrape our dresses and pants and *kurtkas* as we pass by.

Swish, swish.

And the occasional grinding of small stones underfoot, and a smell of forest rot. As we move deeper in, the floor grows softer and the clean smell of astringent pine surrounds us. We push away drooping boughs. The moving line up ahead no longer makes any sound as the growth clears out. When Little Natan starts to whine, he is quickly shushed and picked up by Auntie Maya.

We walk until Kwasova seems very far away. My shoulders begin to relax. I did not realize how tense I have been, knowing those who hunt are behind me. The Cohan brothers had talked of people fleeing through fields, shot in the back as they tried to escape the *Aktions*. My back had all along been ready for a bullet. I roll my neck and shake my arms to loosen the knots.

The sounds of wood jays and nuthatches and song sparrows waking up overhead signals we are nearing the cabin. And then there it is, the ramshackle forestry station we will now call home.

Papa lights a lantern. In the gloom, we see a shelter built from the forest around us. The logs still have rough bark on them, the gaps are stuffed with moss. There is no visible window, just a front door made of smaller logs that closes with the help of a wood latch. If anyone wants to break in, they won't need to. There is no lock.

Papa opens the door, and we slowly gather inside in a group, the two families in the center of the one-room cabin. The cabin is longer than it is wide. If those of us on the outside of the family circle reached out our arms, we would touch a side wall. Along these outer walls, benches are built for sleeping. An iron stove sits on a large flat stone in the left front corner.

There is nothing else.

Auntie Maya starts to cry, and Mama puts an arm around her.

Uncle Levi looks up at the high roofline. "We could build a partial loft for storage." But we have no tools with us yet. He and Papa are to go back to town the next night to get the rest of what we couldn't carry, which includes axes, saws, and hammers. The priority tonight had been food and clothing and bedding, and, of course, us.

As night leaves, I notice a square of light near the stove. It's a kind of window. You can't see out of it—there's no glass. It is made of the same log material as the walls. You have to prop it open with a stick to allow light in, but at least we have something we will be able to open when it's warm enough, something to let out the smoke from the stove when it builds up.

"There's a window, Auntie Maya," I say, tugging on her arm and pointing. She smiles down at me, showing her deep dimples in the lantern light. It is a start.

Exhausted, we find places to lie down on the dirty floor and on the few wall benches. When I lie down next to Leeba and Symon, I am too tired to care that there are dry black mouse droppings and nibbled shells of acorns by my head. We are all together and as far away as we can get from Hitler and his orders to make the land *Judenfrei*.

We sleep through most of the day.

There is much to do when we wake up in late afternoon. We begin by cleaning out the shelter. Mama had packed a hand broom, which we attach to a solid tree branch. She sweeps the floor clear of droppings and the walls and corners clear of cobwebs. The men do not yet dare to saw down any trees until it grows dark, but they gather dry fallen wood for the stove and get it working, after removing an old bird's nest from the stove vent. Then they bank the fire till after dusk, when they will start it up again.

A small stream runs past the house, in a fern-covered gully. With a water source, we know we can survive. It is not large enough to bathe in, holds no fish, but we can get a bucket full of icy clear water for drinking, cooking, and hand bathing.

Before it grows dark, we hang blankets across the middle of the cabin, so that our cousins have the right side of the cabin, and we have the left side. We gather in the front, near the door and the stove, to eat some cold cabbage soup with onions and fennel in it. No one leaves anything in their wood bowls, not even the old gray translucent cabbage. Not liking or not wanting to eat a food is no longer an option. We eat whatever we have. And going hungry by choice is no longer an option. We don't know when our next meal will come. We know that only experienced foresters and hardened resistance fighters live here; we know winters in the backwoods with subzero temperatures are hard to survive.

After supper, and when it is dark enough, the men leave for the second round of supplies. It is the start of many temporary good-byes between them and us women and children. Each time the men are to venture out for something we need—wood, olive oil (it is impossible to find or make *schmaltz* now), washing powder, food, information—it is a ceremony of farewell. Mama always blows Papa his special kiss, and he always holds it to his heart.

We don't know if they will return. And it isn't just the German army we are afraid of, but the bears that come down from the mountains before they start their hibernation, famished and feasting, or the lynx and wild pigs that could injure a leg.

Another cabin to the west is filled with our friends, lucky friends, the Stadnicks and the Rabinowitzes. Gradually during the winter, after forays into the town and to Yuri's place, we hear bits and pieces of stories of the last of our Jewish community, who just disappeared into the forest with only the clothes on their backs and a rucksack. They scattered as far as they could go to avoid being found. The strongest of them built underground bunkers, or joined the partisan armies in the mountains. The weakest didn't make it. But as Papa often says, it is still better to die on your own, free in the woods, then at the hand of the hunter.

Except for the Cohan brothers, the very last of the Jews in our *shtetele,* who were incapable of leaving or afraid to do so (it takes courage to leave what you know, as bad as it can be), were all ordered to move to the Borszczów ghetto on October twenty-second, just ten days after we escaped.

Kwasova is now considered *Judenfrei.*

It is Mama's job to calm the young children before they sleep. Symon and Leeba each snuggle under her arms, and Olena, my oldest cousin at age eight, and Golda, age six, sit in front. Little Natan, just over a year, is usually already asleep in Auntie Maya's arms. We still burn candles, so the light flickers in a jar next to us and illuminates the dark rafters, and the stove's heat fills the cabin. Auntie Maya likes the candles because, she says, it keeps the demons away. Drowsy and warm, we listen to Mama's stories from the Bible and the folktales she grew up with, stories of ice maidens and talking birds and forest animals, even lowly frogs.

Tell me a story . . .

Mama: "There once was a little frog, green and black. He loved adventure and went looking for it every day. This one day, he came upon a bucket made of wood. He jumped up to see what was in it. Below was something that looked like white water. He jumped in to see what it was like. It felt cool and smooth against his green and black skin. He kicked around in it till he was tired. It was time to go home. But he was trapped. He could not get out of the bucket. He could not climb it, and could not reach the bottom to use his frog legs to jump out of it. Was he going to drown? He refused to give up. He kept kicking and swimming, trying to think of a way to get out, somehow, anyhow. He went left, right, around and around, and just as he was about to sink from exhaustion, he kicked again. Finally—he felt something. He pushed his legs down and jumped! He had swum so much he had churned the milk into butter! So never give up, children. Don't ever stop trying to live. Things happen we can't explain or plan sometimes. Our actions are all leading to something else."

I listen while I lean against the rough bark wall and, when she is done talking and the other children are asleep, my mind travels over to the other cabin. I wonder what Leon is doing. Leon with his green eyes. I imagine him sketching some sort of forest creature by their stove. Would he be thinking of me? And I try to picture Alla in her cheery cottage, though at this hour she would be snoring under her patchwork quilt. Maybe the dog is sleeping on the floor next to her, keeping her company. I hope Ovid is not too lonely for Symon, not feeling like we abandoned him. And I try not to think about the way I turned away from Alla's hug when we said good-bye. It leaves me queasy.

Alla will take good care of Ovid. She takes good care of everything and everyone in her life. I hope her age keeps her safe as well. The hard truth is that our leaving is the best thing for her. She can no longer be accused of helping us. Before we left, I put the decorative cross she had lent us in a burlap bag and left it by the chicken coop for her to find the next day.

We go to our new assigned spots on the floor and benches, blow out the candle, and fall asleep in a cleaner, cozier place than the night before. There is hope growing in the mossy cracks and the distant space above the rafters. We can stretch out, unlike in the attic bunkers, and move and eat and live almost normally.

Well, at least live with a new normal. The old normal life of the *shtetele*, with spring festivals and market trading days and school and worship, is as far away as the Carpathian Mountains.

We begin to shift to a different timeframe, one where we sleep in the day and cook and eat at night, so the smoke from our stove won't be visible to anyone who might be fishing or hunting in these woods. We become grateful there is no real window to show our candle and lantern light, and hang a flour sack over the one near the stove so no light shows through the small cracks. There are different demons out there, human demons, that are attracted rather than repulsed by the light.

The shift in sleeping times helps me. I always had trouble sleeping at night anyway, so now I sleep easily in the day and can be wide awake at night.

I love the night, too. Mama lets me and Leeba and Symon and Olena, the older children who know how not to make much noise, wander outside under the moonlight, as long as we don't go far from the cabin's clearing. We also have to be careful not to leave obvious signs. No drawing in the pine needles and dirt, no piles of stones. The younger ones usually play house under the dense umbrellas of the fir trees' lower branches, and I have started to study our new surroundings.

Alla says that nature is a map, so I try to read the forest.

I explore clearings, a hollow tree. I poke at fallen, rotten tree trunks. Even when dead, I learn, the forest provides food and life to other things. Moss and small tree saplings grow in the moist crevices of the "nurse" logs, as Papa calls them. And colorful mushrooms—white, brown, yellow. They are delicious fried with wild garlic.

I learn that light moves and dances in the forest. It's never stable as in the steppe lands. In the forest, you can't take light, even moonlight, for granted. It keeps changing and moving out of your grasp.

I visit the same places each day, and watch life change. New green on the ends of hemlocks that look like little gloved hands. Pinecones appearing like brown jewelry on branches. Hardwood leaves starting to lose their green, letting other colors trickle through their leaf veins till they are full of yellow, orange, red. Then they let go gradually, and fall to the forest floor. In my mind, as I watch them fall, I see images of men, women, and children falling into ravines.

So many things can happen to a leaf. It can get chewed up. It can fall into a small stream and get washed to sea or rot in a tidal pool. It can be gathered up by squirrels and other animals as nest lining, and spend its winter under some warm furry belly. It can grow a fungus. Or it can lie where it fell, or where someone or something kicked it, and go dark and dusty and seep back into the soil.

That is, if it's left alone. As I read the woods, I realize that if nothing interferes with the path of an object or a living thing, the possibilities of where it could go are many.

While listening to the cuckoos as they fly from pine to pine, and while watching the jays and squirrels bury acorns before twilight, I get the idea to make little *motanky* dolls for the children. Olena and Golda had been told to leave their dolls behind.

Being a bit older than the rest, and beyond playing their games, I usually take on the role of supervisor. But sometimes, while they play soccer indoors with a rock, or stickball with a mushroom, I now hunt for shiny acorns. There are many oak trees in the deep forest, and birds and animals transfer the nuts around and bury them not very well or drop them from the trees above. I kick around the forest bracken and carpets of needles, looking for the small shine of captured moonlight on a tiny dark globe.

Back in the cabin, we sort them for roasting. Some have tiny holes in them from worms that got to the nut inside before we did. I take some of the bad ones aside and use a sharp sewing needle to carve a face into the brown skin of the shell. The ones found with their caps still attached become men, and for women, I glue on some moss hair with melted candle wax and tie thick but tender green leaves as head scarves around their nut heads. The bodies are made from rolled birch bark, and tough dry June grass becomes twine to create the outstretched arms. We can't afford to use any scrap material for clothes, so I use the leaf husks we rip off of the dry corn we occasionally get when we trade. Even Leeba and Symon want one, and help make doll furniture from round starry nettle seeds that stick together to form chairs and tables. Then they join in reenacting the folktales they hear before bedtime. Or they play "market" and haggle over pretend wares. When the games turn to war, we stop them.

Golda becomes so attached to her *motanky* dolls, she sleeps with them at night.

In the back of my head, I hear Alla's voice: "Every year, the serpent sends out his minions to check on us."

I figure that if there is a serpent, I might not be making eggs, but maybe the acorns will work. They look like small chestnut eggs.

I start to decorate them in the way that Alla decorates her eggs. On the backs of their heads, I draw symbols of oak leaves for strength, and wheat stalks to keep us healthy. We are terrified of one of us getting sick in such a small space, as surely everyone would get sick then. With no doctor in the area, it could be a death sentence. We make sure to bathe every day with buckets of water.

And I hope the wheat stalk etchings will help.

Mama and Papa ignore what I'm doing. The symbols are not from our culture. Papa picked up a *motanky* doll one day and saw the carvings at the back of the head. He didn't know exactly what they were, but he looked at me darkly. I looked away, a little scared he would be angry, but he put down the doll. I know he doesn't approve—Jews are not to desecrate their bodies with marks or tattoos, and I have heard Mama grumble many times about her not wanting her daughter to create graven images—but I feel I am doing the right thing in this new space we are in, a space that has a life of its own.

Papa singles me out for his confidence, on the day he is preparing for a trip to the *shtetele* to get flour and kerosene from the Cohan brothers. We've been out of both for two weeks, and have been snowed into our cabin. It is early in December. The drifts pile more than halfway up the front door that opens out. When the weather got cold we made an indoor corner for bathing, which we now use as a toilet area, too. It is uncomfortable going in a bucket so close to people, but we have no choice. We are going hardly at all, anyway, as we aren't eating much. Uncle Levi hangs out the window and digs a snow pit to the right of it to empty the slops. On a warmer day, he will remove the partially frozen waste to a far-off clearing and bury it.

When the snow melts enough to push open the front door, Papa gets ready to leave with snowshoes and a birch bark face mask to protect himself against the icy snow crystals that could cut his face. He has not gone to Kwasova since it started snowing, afraid of leaving tracks that would lead others back. But we are starving. All our pickles are eaten, our bread, sugar beets, dumplings, soup, and stashed acorns. All that is left are dried berries, wild onions, and some oats. Without kerosene, we have only a small supply of candles.

Little Natan cries most of the day and night now. Tired, weak cries.

Papa has to go and risk leaving snow tracks. Perhaps the night winds will cover his line of passage back into the forest.

Uncle Levi stays behind. In case Papa is captured, at least one man will be left to care for us. So Mama looks at Papa sharply when he tells me to put on my *kurtka*, Uncle's snow shoes and bark mask, and Leeba's scarf.

"She's not going with me, Eva, not to worry. But I need to show her something before I leave." She tilts her head in agreement, then lifts the thick collar of his *kurtka* and kisses him on the mouth. While kisses in the past were quick little moments, or blown, this one lingers. The rest of us look away.

We pull down our masks, and I follow Papa through the drifts of blue-white snow. The moon is out tonight, not good for Papa, but he also needs the moon because if it is out, that means the stars are out. And he needs the moon to show him where to go and the stars to tell him when daylight is coming. When the Big Dipper turns on its handle, we learn morning soon follows. Like Alla had preached, we are all reading the world like a new map.

I know the *shtetele* is straight out from the front door, so am surprised when he veers left. We walk through the forest, and the cold wet snow flips up my skirt with the flapping of the snow shoes. But I don't complain. I know something important is happening.

We cross a deer trail, and tracks that look like they are from a lynx. Not many animals but a lynx could stay on top of the deep snow with its soft wide pads. We know we are not alone in these woods, and I wonder if animals are watching us right now. A shiver runs down my spine, even though I know the bears are sleeping this time of year. I glance around for the glow of green cat eyes from under a bush.

The air is so cold, it freezes into sparkling crystals that fly around, as if winged.

Just at that moment, something large and dark and silent swoops across our path.

"That's a Long-eared owl." Papa looks back at me through the eye holes of his mask and points at the silhouette receding into the pines. "They make no noise when they fly so they can hear their prey. We have to be like the owl, silent."

It had made no noise, but it flew so close to me I could sense the air being shifted by its wings.

We begin to go over a slight hill, then down on the other side.

The moon makes the top of the snow sparkle. It is like a magical winter wonderland in Mama's tales. Black branch shadows reach and twist about against the white landscape. Then we come to a stop. Papa is at the base of a large tree that grows out of the downward side of the hill. It is a tree I have never seen before. Its bark is smooth and light gray and its trunk is about two feet wide. Naked branches spread out and intermingle with the greenery of the pines and spruce that surround it.

"This is a beech tree," he says, patting its bark with his woolen mitten. "Look on the other side."

I walk around the tree. There I find markings carved into the bark, about five feet up. The flesh of the tree is dark, so the marks stand out against the gray skin. I see concentric circles and marks and arrows and an X.

It is a secret language.

"This is what my fellow shepherds and foresters call a Witness Tree. It is how they have communicated to each other for centuries. Out in the forest-steppe alone . . . they leave these little signs on beech trees, some lodgepole pines, birches, aspens. Any tree that has a light bark that can be carved into, so the carving shows up. It is a way to say you exist in the wilderness, a way to know someone else is out here with you. It is also a way to leave messages about weather and conditions and possible dangers." He hesitates. Then rubs his mittens against the signs. "The forester who is helping us, Yuri, is using this tree. I have let him know there are ten of us in his cabin"—he points to two sets of four vertical marks with one horizontal mark drawn through each group—"and he has let me know that so far there have been no sightings of Germans in the forest. See this mark?" He points to the X, which is within a square box just below the ten marks.

"I check this now and then for anything from him. You can trust him, Hanna. If something happens to me, I want you to keep this going. You don't need to know anything special. This is one of those times that the Torah prepares us for, when we must go against our traditions. I, like you, have taken to drawing these stick lines to protect us. You have my permission to carve on the tree if necessary. Just try to disguise somehow what you must say to him."

My stomach feels knotted at the possibility of losing Papa. I start to fully cry for the first time since the *Aktions* started. In an instant, my tears drop down behind the mask and freeze on Leeba's scarf. They form into little glass beads. Papa pulls me close and hugs me. His warmth melts them into the wool.

I don't want to let go. But I have to.

"It is fine to cry, Hanna," he says, while I keep gulping to hold back the tears. "Crying is a form of breathing."

"Why me and not Uncle Levi?" I ask, recovering.

"You seem to enjoy carving and symbols, and I need someone who, if she is caught, has a chance at survival."

I look up at him questioningly.

"Your youth and your blond hair . . ."

That statement lies heavy in the air. Once again I am somehow separate from the family because of this legacy that's been passed down to just me and Symon.

Then a sound like several small dogs barking comes from above, making me jump. Papa points up into the pine tree overhang. It takes me a minute to see what he is pointing to. Many dark silhouettes stand out in the branches, some with glowing orange eyes looking down on us.

"That's the Long-eared owl's alarm call. In the winter, the owls roost together for protection."

Just as we do, I think.

I see an owl feather on the snow below one of the trees, and pick it up. It is a tawny color, mixed with white and black streaks meant to camouflage the bird against tree bark. *I wish we had skin that could camouflage us, so the Germans could walk right on by and not see us.*

"Why don't people have camouflage?" I ask Papa.

"Because we have weapons and minds," he says quietly. "And because we don't yet know we are supposed to get along."

We make our way silently back to the cabin, where I leave him to his mission. Before he goes, he says, "Don't worry about me, Hanna. The Talmud says walking in moonlight is like walking with a companion. I won't be alone."

I watch his back retreat into the darkness.

Inside the warm cabin, I shake off the snow just inside the door. Mama doesn't question, just takes my coat and the scarf and hangs them to dry by the stove. My skirt and tights are wet, and I feel heavy with responsibility.

Papa has been gone for four days. The children are hungry and bickering. Uncle Levi tries to get their minds off their stomachs and shows them how to play a Passover game with some of the unripe green acorns that fell too early, which we can't eat, called *Um tsi grod?* Odd or even? Little Natan can't be distracted, but the rest join in and quiz each other on whether or not they are holding in their hands an odd or even number.

Symon is very competitive and pouts when Leeba guesses correctly—"Even!"—and he has to put his handful back in the *kon*, the circle from which the players first picked them up. Eventually he wins, and he struts around the cabin like a vain rooster. Leeba throws an acorn at him and they mock wrestle until Mama breaks them apart.

I keep track of time on the inside cover of my book by Mr. Twain. Once in a while, someone will ask me what day it is. It is easy to lose track of time in one room you never leave, away from normal routines, and Papa has the only watch. We have to use the sun to frame each day.

I find a beech tree in the Joan of Arc story as well. A fairy tree. A mystical tree connected to the children of Domrémy, the hamlet that she grew up in. I feel like I am following in her footsteps. I tear another thin strip of notepaper and copy the passage.

I am also half-listening to Mama tell a story, trying not to dwell on my grumbling belly and Little Natan's whining, when we hear muffled sounds and the door opens with a rush of cold air.

"Papa!" my brother and sister and I shout.

"Uncle Abram!" my cousins squeal. He is surrounded by the children, all jumping on him and pulling at his clothes.

He laughs and drops a large sack on the floor with a *thump*, and brings in another sack from a sled outside.

It's a Friday night, Papa tells us, dawning into Saturday. Another thing the war has taken away from us—our customs. We can't survive in the winter forest without lighting a match on Saturday. We have no Shabbes goy to do it for us, and we have given up trying to start the stove with tinder. Papa cannot bring himself to do it, but Uncle Levi steps forward and quietly does the task so we won't freeze. While we sleep we can get away with no stove on, because we lie so closely together it takes time for the heat to escape through the cabin cracks. But by evening, when the sun starts to go down behind the tree line, we begin to tremble uncontrollably and have to light the stove. In Kwasova, it can go to thirty degrees below zero on a winter's night.

"Let's cook quickly, before we have to put out the stove. Look what I brought back!" He holds up a skinned, half-frozen chicken. "Ivan Umański gave me flour and a chicken killed the kosher way. He said he had it frozen for us, waiting till I might come back. He got it from . . ." He stops. Osip the Butcher was one of our neighbors turned in before we left. He is rumored to be in the Borszczów ghetto, with other Kwasovians who had been caught and not killed during the Sukkōt raid.

"This is a special chicken. We may not have any other meat for weeks. Or months."

Soon the cabin is filled with the smell of chicken boiling on the stove. Our mouths water and our stomachs growl in unison for the coming taste of chicken and dumpling soup. Some of the fat is saved to make a bit of *schmaltz*. Mama leaves a little fat on the chicken because she says we need all we can get in our bellies.

We pray for Osip the Butcher, and for Ivan Umański, who put off his own need for meat to help sustain our family. Both men helped keep us alive that winter. One good meal can go a long way.

We eat very slowly. It is not good on the body to eat too much too fast after going without.

When the last bones are licked, we put them aside for later. We are so giddy with full bellies and moist, tasty meat. Papa and Uncle Levi begin to sing and dance the *freylekhs*. We clap hands and move about in a circle while they pass a handkerchief back and forth in the center. They pretend to dual in a dance like Cossack soldiers, trying to do it in a funny way to make the children laugh. The attempt to be energetic and lively doesn't last long—we are too weak—but I haven't seen dancing or joy in what feels like forever.

The rest of the children fall asleep easily, even Little Natan, as daylight creeps in beneath the front door. But the food and song and dance have made my sluggish body vibrate with life, and I can't lie still. The stove is now out, and I hear the adults talking next to it. I crawl over to hear what they are saying. When you're hidden away, with no freedom, you crave news of the outside world as much as you crave food.

"They are taking away railway cars full of Jews, the cars we once used for cattle. They say they are taking them to the Land of Israel." That statement hangs in the air. By now, we do not believe anything the Germans say.

"Pavel said it is a matter of time before their badges will be taken away and they will no longer be allowed to move about freely. They have salvaged tons of metal. It is piling up in the barn, but no one is collecting it. Therefore, they may need our protection soon. We have so little room as it is . . . I think they can move into the other cabin. Oh, and Sonia Rabinowitz is pregnant," he says to Mama, who gasps. She exchanges a look with her sister. The look seems to say, how could anyone bring a child into this world? The idea now seems frightening.

I want to know how Leon is doing, but decide since nothing bad is being reported beyond the pregnancy in the other cabin, all must be well. But how are they faring without the meat we just had? Especially a pregnant woman.

"Typhus is spreading throughout the cities, *shteteles*, and villages, spread by the German army. Another evil they are bringing. They blame the Jews for being carriers, of course, because they have crowded them into terrible conditions in the camps and ghettoes, so they become covered in lice. And lice bring typhus."

I remember the poster in the bakery window.

"Sounds like we are almost better off here in the woods," Uncle Levi says. "We are lucky we had the Cohan brothers to warn us about not going to the ghettoes."

Papa pulls on his beard. "Yes, you could say that. People from the ghettoes are being deported as well. I fear to their death. Though we do need to keep a watch for partisan fighters. They are getting hungry, too, and coming down from the mountains." His eyes take on a fierce glow. "But we are all together. Many families have separated in their flight. Whatever happens, we must all stay together."

His eyes look at each one of the adults. They each nod in return.

"There may come a time when we have to leave this place. I will keep checking for messages from Yuri. I can no longer visit him in person. It is not safe either to go back to the *shtetele*. Some Ukrainian and Polish neighbors are pillaging Jewish homes and taking the furniture and clothing. They will turn any Jew in."

"Is it time to leave Ukraine? Could we get out?" Uncle Levi asks. "I heard some left for Canada just as the war began."

Papa shakes his head. "We would not get out of this country alive right now. There are too many of us and the countryside is now crawling with SS and Gestapo agents, who are paying young Ukrainian boys to go into the fields and forests to find Jews."

Already the joy of the night is disappearing with the dawn. I crawl back to my spot and lie on the hard floor, my shoulder blades and hip bones sore. Why us? Why do the Germans and many of our own neighbors hate us so much? We never do anything to hurt them. We keep to ourselves. We don't fight.

I think of the stories the Cohans have passed on of Jews marching to trenches and standing next to them, waiting to be shot. A few tried to run away.

I decide that if that were to happen to me, I would be the one to run. As far as I could and as fast as I could, even if a bullet came anyway. I would want to die under my own terms, with some last glimmer of hope for escape, looking far away into the distance, not into a finite ditch, but as far away as I could from the evil behind me.

But I do not have a child to protect or depend on me. My last thought, before I say the Shema, is of the young mother Jacob told us about, while he choked on his own tears—a mother who smothered her own child in her winter coat before the shot came, so the child would not feel the bullet.

The chicken bones are boiled for soup, the bones picked of their marrow, even the gristle chewed by the men.

We miss the taste.

The smell hangs in the cabin for two days, taunting us.

Gradually the taste of meat becomes a memory once again, as Uncle Levi tries to set up some snares without much knowledge of how to make them work, and they remain empty.

Days tick by.

Tick ... Tick ...

I mark the inside cover of my book, read more about Joan's crusade, and the children play with their *motanky* dolls.

From the outside looking in, we could be any normal household in the town of Kwasova, only we are isolated and without the daily freedom to make of our lives what *we* want. We have to focus on survival. We hunt for anything edible that might have survived winter, even the withered berries that grow on the wild grapevines that weave and tangle themselves into the landscape. They have a bitter aftertaste, but a few are enough to keep you from fainting.

The line between hunger and starvation is that thin.

I am beginning to realize that freedom means you can be who you are meant to be, whatever that is. That freedom is different for different people. That breathing without any thought to it is a gift.

Now, I think about breathing all the time. What is it like to take your last breath? What if the sound of it gave you away?

A sound.

What was that?

Slowly waking up.

A knock on the door.

Papa and Uncle Levi, who lie closest to the front of the cabin, grab their axes and jump to either side of the door.

The knock comes again, more hesitant this time.

What could the men do? It's a flimsy wood door that anyone could kick in. They open it slowly.

The rest of us freeze on the floor, too terrified to move.

Outside, in the cloudy light, stands an older man, bent over in cold mist, pulling all his clothes around him.

It was inevitable that at least one of the Kwasovians from the valley who fled into the woods would find us.

But it's a shock to us all when Uncle Levi slowly asks, with uncertainty in his voice, "Fedir Wolinski?"

Mr. Wolinski—Fedir the Lamplighter—who had become a *Tzeler* and betrayed us all, especially Symon, his former friend.

The men look about the clearing, as if fearful of seeing an army behind him. But he is alone, disheveled and shaking. When he recognizes us, his eyes go wide and dark and he steps back as if hit. Then he turns to melt back into the hazy morning. He stumbles in the snow and falls to his knees with no cry.

Mama gets up from the floor and goes to Papa. I do not see her face, as it is turned away from us, but I see Papa look down on her and his expression go soft. She puts a hand on his sleeve. I know they are talking without saying words. They have a way of doing that more and more these days. I guess when you are married for a long time, you don't need them.

Papa goes out and lifts Mr. Wolinski up by the armpits and drags him back into the cabin. The lamplighter, who walked our night streets for years, can no longer stand up. Thin, scabbed, exhausted, he murmurs something I can't hear in Polish, and they put him down in front of the stove where he sleeps the rest of the day, steam rising from his drying clothes. Our families settle back down to finish our sleep, but I stay awake. There is an enemy in our midst, and Papa with the axe by his side does not settle me enough. I am wary, weak as this enemy is.

I must have dozed off after all, because I wake up to voices. Mr. Wolinski is awake and slurping cold berry soup. He had come upon our cabin while journeying north to Kiev. "I have family there," he says.

Uncle Levi tells him Kiev is not safe either, but the man just nods, slurps more soup. He smells. His clothes are in tatters. He sits on a log stump we use for a seat, and using needle and thread Mama mends what clothes she can while he still wears them.

Symon stays far away in a corner, his arms crossed, with an angry expression on his red face.

"Why are *you* fleeing them?" Papa asks quietly.

Mr. Wolinski sighs. "You had every right to kill me, after the role I took on with the Germans, but I am grateful you are better than I am."

Though his enamel bowl is now empty, he keeps swirling the spoon around the bottom, as if doing so will call up more soup. But Mama has reached her limits of kindness.

"I thought they would save us from Russia. The Russians killed my father and brother. And the Germans paid. It put food on my table. But Hitler's SS are turning on the Polish now, using the Ukrainian police to do their dirty work. They are claiming we are part of the resistance, even if we are not. When my wife screamed at them for taking her silver, they shot *her* on the spot. . . . It is not a safe time for Jews, Poles, or gypsies; even Ukrainians the SS feel are nationalists. If they don't go after you with guns, it is with their vicious guard dogs, trained to kill. And I was warned the SS do not want their Counters alive, once there is nothing left to record. There are to be no witnesses."

We let that news settle in slowly. We are now not alone in our misery. Here is a man who had lit our paths and kept us safe all of his working days, then turned on us to benefit himself. And who is now being fed and helped by the ones he would have betrayed in an instant.

I let that thought roll around my head while I gather dry grass outside. I cut what is above the snow with a knife, gathering handfuls into a bucket, and take the grass back to stuff into the lamplighter's pants and coat, trying not to smell his meaty, acidic body odor. He smells of fear and desperation. I gag a few times.

It is a smell I will always remember.

I fill up the loose parts of clothing. It's an old peasant hunting trick Papa knows about from sheepherding. We can't afford to give away even one blanket, and his chances of freezing to death are high.

He leaves, all puffed up, with a hunk of dry bread. When Mama gives it to him, a bit of moisture runs out of one old rheumy eye and disappears into his white mustache. He tries to give the bread back. She shakes her head and pushes him out the door.

He blesses her, and gives a last sad look to Symon, who turns his back on him.

We will never see the *Tzeler* again.

The dark settles around us as he leaves. We light the stove and huddle around it. No one says a word for a long time. Mr. Woliński is a reminder that there is still a war on, people who still hunt us like prey. It's been easy in the neutral forest to feel protected and embraced by the branches and under-growth. But the hunters are still out there; we, and now others, are still in danger.

But my parents taught me something when they took in the Death Counter.

Life is not good, however you are living it, if you become like those who don't value you.

Our food supply is running low again. Water is not an issue as all we have to do is melt snow on the stove and boil it for a long time, and we fill our growling bellies with as much of it as we can. Mama and Auntie Maya make soup out of whatever we scrape together. Sometimes it's only hot yellow water that they've boiled some inner bark and pine needles in. The children try halfheartedly to play their game of *Um tsi grod?*

Little Natan is starting to cry again. We cover our ears.

We have made it through the darkest part of the winter and are entering into the longer days, so our daylight hours when we sleep get longer, too. Which is good.

What else is there to do, when you are starving, but try to lose yourself in sleep and hope to dream of some delectable food? Like *pyroshki*, cherry turnovers fried so the outside is crisp and crumbles in your mouth and the sweet-sour filling explodes against your tongue like smooth icing. Or the *babka*, so flaky you could peel it off in pieces to expose the delicious nut and poppy seed center. And sweet *matzoh* balls, made with eggs, milk, and sugar and fried till golden. I think I dream most about sweet food because it makes you feel happy when you eat it.

We get lucky. Spring comes early in 1943. I wake feeling warm on what I believe is my birthday, or at least near enough to February twenty-second. I look outside the front door and see that winter appears to be melting away. That means the men can start moving about again more safely, dodging snow piles but managing to keep out of mud so as not to leave behind those treacherous footsteps. And that means they can start making dangerous treks again to find us food.

I have made it to age fifteen. I put a star next to the day mark in my book. I know I won't get gifts this year or a cake, but being alive and with my family is gift enough.

So when Golda and Olena come over to me as I sit on my blanket, I am surprised to see them hold out one of their father's brown heavy wool socks.

"For your special day, Cousin Hanna!" they cry in unison.

I take the sock, puzzled. Something is inside. I hold it upside down and shake, and out drops a sharpened pencil with an eraser.

They beam at me, and Golda, who has freckles over her nose and a lisp, announces proudly, "Iss a pencil!"

I pull her to me gently. She feels so thin, like she could be broken. "It's the best present ever. How did you both know I needed a new one?" I hold up the pencil stub from my dress pocket.

"Olena said you did," Golda declares.

Then Leeba sits next to me and calls for Symon, who comes from the back of the cabin with his hands behind his back.

"Guess which hand?" he smirks. Symon never makes things easy for you.

"Umm, how about the right one?"

"Nah." He holds up an empty right hand.

"All right, the left one?"

Mama and Auntie Maya have joined us now, and watch while he holds out something bright and shiny.

I gasp. It's a gold ring with a red stone in it.

I take it and put it on my middle finger, as it is too large for my index finger.

"That's your bubbe's wedding ring," Mama says gently. "It's the last piece of her jewelry that she refused to sell during the hunger war. She wanted you, her first granddaughter, to have it on your sixteenth birthday, but Maya and I agree you should have it now. It's a ruby, a good one. We need to keep it hidden, but you can wear it today."

Then they both kiss me with dry lips. I can see they are emotional, thinking of their mother, their eyes almost spilling over. I never knew either one of my grandmothers; my bubbe on my mother's side died a few years after I was born, and I never met her. But I have heard many stories of her strength, of how she kept her whole family alive through the Russian pogroms and then the hunger war.

"You remind me of her, Hanna," Mama says softly in my ear, then turns away to go to the stove to start cooking for us.

I follow her and watch her shoulders shake as she stands over the hot iron surface, crying silently, not letting the younger ones see, all the sadness in her shoulders and bent head. From the stories I have heard of my bubbe's strength, I decide my mother is wrong.

She is the one like her mother.

While Papa and Uncle Levi are away, scavenging for food (we are so desperate they decided they had to take a chance and both go out, in different directions), I walk down to Yuri's Witness Tree one clear night to check for messages. Papa had told me he'd left another scratch count for the forester to show Yuri we all made it through the winter.

I am no longer afraid to walk in the dark. Moonlight might be a companion, but darkness and shadows have become my friends. The night covers me like a velvet cloak. And I am no longer afraid of the night animals. They have no wish to harm us if we leave them alone.

I listen to the night birds twittering, the owls barking, the foxes screaming, forest martens scurrying about. We all have the same enemy now, and they no longer are afraid of me, either. They cross my path without even looking, and the Long-eared owls seem to play with me. They swoop in circles above my head, so closely I can see their black talons when there is moonlight.

I love the owls best. I think because I wish I could fly, like they do. Fly far away to a better place.

When I get to the far side of the tree, the pale moonlight shines on a new X. I trace it with my finger, relieved. Our forest is still safe. I look around and see no sign of Yuri, other than this mark.

It is hard to believe we share the woods with this silent sympathizer.

I think there is something in the ancient nature of spring to give everyone, even us, a bit of hope. The snow completely melts from the roof and all around the cabin, but for some grainy grayish patches left under trees where the sun can't reach, marred with brown spots from the squirrels above.

We gather pine catkins from low branches, pick off the papery covers, and chew on these nutty treats. We feel better with more food in our bellies.

No partisan fighters have shown up in our part of the forest, and the children are allowed to play for short periods again in the clearing. Papa says he will make a trek to the Stadnick cabin to share some supplies. My ears perk up when I hear this.

Olena saved one of her own books, which has endpapers. I ask if I she can spare one. She tears it off.

I take my birthday pencil and the thick paper out to the mushroom log. Sitting in the clearing, the sounds of squirrels chattering at me and nuthatches chirping, their talons clicking against bark as they explore the pine trees, I write him:

Dear Leon:
[I sit for a while, not knowing what to say after this.
Dear Leon, Dear Leon.]

I hope you and your family are getting along well. We are managing. I love the forest.

I made it to 15. I even got some gifts. I am thinking of you and your 17th birthday. By then, I hope I will have something to give you besides a simple letter.

I hope I see you again. ~~I miss you~~
[I decide to erase this part.]

[*How should I sign?*]

~~Love from~~ [erase]

~~Faithfully yours~~ [erase]

Your Friend,

Hanna

I fold it up many times into a tight square.

Back at the cabin, I give it to Papa. I feel myself blush. He barely looks at it or me and puts it in his *kurtka* pocket.

It is hard to keep my mind off the letter while he is gone. I sweep the cabin, give Little Natan a bath in the clearing, the moonlight shimmering off of his small pale body. He shivers in the cool spring night air, and I wrap him in a blanket when we are done. He giggles. What a beautiful sound, I think, better than all his crying.

How good it feels to hold life in your arms.

I have trouble sleeping the next day. I keep picturing Leon opening the multiple folds till he gets to the note. *Should I have written what I did? Will he laugh at me? Did I make a mistake?*

My legs won't stop moving. Leeba kicks me at one point, frustrated. I force myself to lie still after that, and eventually slip into sleep.

Two short knocks on the door, a pause, then three more.

Papa is back!

"They are all well. But Sonia is very thin. She says she feels the baby move, however, so that is a good sign."

Papa hands me folded paper. It is thick, like mine was. Leon has sent me a note on an endpaper ripped from a book, too!

I feel myself turning red again. I hate turning red. Feeling my face burn, it gets even redder. To get away from the others so I can read it privately, I walk down to the beech tree.

Spring snow, like white puddles, sprinkles the undergrowth. In one snow patch, I see the outline of a bird of prey, an owl or a hawk. Tiny round prints lead away from it, or toward it, more likely. It is a carved photolike impression of the moment of capture, left behind in the granular ice.

Maybe this is the way of the world, I wonder, to always have something bigger than you hunting you down.

At that moment, I hear something on my right that stops me short and sends my head buzzing with alarm. It is a sound I have not heard in a while. A loud crackling in the undergrowth. Heart racing, I hide behind a maple trunk.

A herd of small roe deer move through. I take a few breaths before moving on. Deer are quiet hopping about in the snow. In the brush, they make more noise.

When I get to the beech tree, I sink down at the foot of it and pull out my note, my heart beating fast, still from fear but now also from excitement.

Dear Hanna,

I promise to make it to 17. Around your birthday, I thought of you.

I think you must be keeping the German army away.

My cousins perished during Purim. They were shot in their cemetery. They were found hiding in a bunker. The Germans are finding the bunkers now. It is good we left.

I miss them. I can't help but wonder, what good did it do for the world to have them gone?

I pray I see you again, too.

Your Friend,

Leon

Under his name is a drawing of what looks like a little fox. It is prancing across the bottom of the page, leaving footprints in the snow behind it.

I read the note about ten times. How far away our schoolyard seems, and our childhood. I am only fifteen, but I feel much older. I started menstruating when I was thirteen, but nothing came this winter; I am too thin and hungry, Mama says. It is hard to believe I am old enough to have a baby. But given the chance, no matter how good it feels to hold one, I would not bring a child into this new world. It is too hateful. I wonder again how Sonia could.

But the fact he wrote to me cheers me up. I feel special—special because Leon used some precious paper and wrote me a note and took the time to draw me something from the forest that is now our home. Maybe he sees the woods as I do, a special protective place, and the animals as our friends.

I sigh, and put the letter away in my pocket. I almost leave without checking the far side of the tree, but when I stand, using the rough trunk behind me to rise from the ground reminds me to take a look.

It takes me moments to process what I see.

Underneath the X that I had seen last month . . .

. . . is a large O in a box.

An O!

Meaning the Germans are in the forest! Somewhere, Yuri has spied on them. I touch the curvature of the O, and it's still sticky.

It's a brand-new carving.

I run. I don't feel the brambles tearing my clothes or slicing my hands and shins. When I trip on a log, I get up and run again even faster. I hear the children now, near the cabin, laughing and squealing. Making noise that can be heard far and wide. Alerting all to our presence.

We have become too comfortable.

We gather everyone into the cabin and put out the stove. We blow out candles and lamp wicks. Papa leaves immediately with an axe and a knife to make the dangerous trip through the forest several miles to go find Yuri before the sun comes up, his face blackened with stove soot so it won't shine white under the stars. He is learning partisan survival tactics from the peasants he trades with, and uses them now.

We can't eat. We sit and cling to each other, staring into space, jumping when something falls on the metal roof with a *clang* that we normally ignore. When the soft sounds of squirrel feet patter above, we breathe again.

Our time in the sheltering forest has ended.

While we wait for Papa to return the next day, we can't sleep, but for the younger children who collapse, exhausted from being told to keep quiet, their thumbs in their mouths.

After a night of numbness, Mama rises and orders the rest of us to scramble and pack. We are ready now to move in an instant. We eat some winter pears that Uncle Levi had traded firewood for, and drink cold creek water.

The sun begins to lower, and Papa returns and wipes his face clean.

"I need you to go to the other cabin," he tells Uncle Levi. "Tell them to pack all their belongings and to bury what they can so that it looks like no one was staying there, then bring them to our cabin tomorrow night. Do not travel when the sun is up. The Germans know there are hideaways in the forest and are starting to search deeper in the day, when they can see, now that the snow is gone. They want to give Hitler a birthday present of ridding the country of as many Jews as they can find, and there are more of the SS now stationed in Kwasova, so they are feeling braver about running into any resistance fighters. We have very little time."

Uncle Leon nods, grabs his *kurtka* and hat and a spike, gives his wife and sister-in-law and children a kiss. I have never seen him kiss anyone but my aunt.

Then he is gone, the door banging with his exit.

My father has dark circles under his eyes, and for the first time, I notice gray around his temples and in his beard. It's as if the gray erupted overnight. Now both my parents have gray in their hair. It scares me.

He slumps onto a bench. Mama kneels and removes his boots. We all keep quiet. We wait for him to speak.

He sits straighter, then, "Yuri said we must leave. That the Germans and their dogs will find us in a few days, maybe sooner, if we do not. They are no longer taking prisoners or taking Jews to camps. They are shooting those in the forest and in the fields on sight. Then they are taking their clothes and possessions back to the town and selling them."

I remember the ruby ring, sewn safely again into my mother's dress hem.

"They are no longer allowing those with badges to roam free, either. The Cohans are no longer safe. They are being asked to register as Jews with the police, who are issuing *kennkarten* to all remaining Jews who were allowed to work in our district. The yellow cards have photos and names and are marked with a red *J* for Jews. Some Ukrainians are beginning to blackmail anyone who is hiding as a non-Jew or refusing to register. We have to get word to those boys so they can find us before they are taken or shot."

"But where can we go, Abram?" Mama asks with some panic in her voice.

"I need some food and water."

She scurries over to the stove and brings him back some creek water from the tin bucket, then breaks off a piece of black bread and slices a hard pear.

We watch while he eats. When he is done, he wets his finger, picks up each bread crumb from his shirt, and brings his finger to his mouth. He sighs when there are no more crumbs, then puts his hands on his thighs and speaks firmly.

"I have to go look right now. Down in the valley, to the northeast, is a hollow in a farmer's field. Yuri says there is a cave down there."

My mother and aunt gasp.

"I know," he continues, holding up his hand like he is warding off their reaction. "It sounds bad, doesn't it? But what choice do we have? We will not survive living deeper in the woods. We will be shot if we stay here. Yuri has been down the cave once and says it is large enough for everyone from both cabins. If we all stay together and work together to make it livable, it just might get us through all of this."

Auntie Maya cries out, "But there are evil spirits in caves, we cannot go down there! And with the *children*!" Her face is ghostly white, her eyes round and dark with fear.

My mother puts her arm around her younger sister. "Maya . . . the evil is up here, not down in the caves," she says gently.

I shiver. It feels like something cold blew in.

And that is how we all came to hide in the gypsum caves of Kwasova, where darkness is even darker than night.

The Caves

For she was in a black dungeon . . . for she was in a cage. . . . She had been in that cage a long time now, but not long enough to break her spirit.

—COPIED BY HANNA SLIVKA
FROM "TRIAL AND MARTYRDOM," CHAPTER III

THE REUNION BETWEEN the two cabins is warm, but muted. The urgency of moving faster than the Germans are moving keeps us from celebrating when the Stadnicks and Rabinowitzes enter the cabin with their packs.

Their clothes hang loosely on them, faded and worn at the cuffs and hems, and their faces have aged and sagged. I wonder if we look the same way to them.

Leon's eyes move across the adults embracing, and find mine. I blush, smile, feel my stomach hop at the eye contact. He is taller, and his mother has lengthened his black pants and sleeves with a brown material. He has a bit of scruff on his chin, a new beard beginning. In another situation he would have looked clownish. To me, in that forest hovel held together with moss and mud, he looks like a handsome prince. I am too shy to greet him physically (when did I become so shy around Leon?), so stand back while Leeba runs around the adults and hugs him for me.

We are ready to move on, as ready as we can be.

The cabin has been swept and we will leave nothing behind. All items we do not want to carry, we buried. We even clogged the stovepipe back up after airing the room out to get rid of our smells, and sprinkled pine needles around the wood floor and old acorn bits the squirrels had discarded. We wanted to leave no trace behind, wanted it to look unused, so as not to alert our pursuers that there were recent survivors in the area.

Each child was told they could bring one *motanky* doll. There was no way to carry more. With sadness, we'd had a little burial ceremony for the unwanted ones the day before. We wrapped the dolls in shrouds of new green leaves. I could not help but think of friends and neighbors as we shoveled dirt over the acorn figures. That real people were being discarded with less care than these dry dolls. We left a few stones as grave markers on the surface and I recited Kaddish, a mourners' prayer that men recite after a death. The women had been allowed to recite it, from our synagogue balcony, along with the men seated below, and since I was the oldest, I recited the prayer as best as I could remember: ". . . *Oseh shalom bim'romav hu ya'aseh shalom, . . .* He Who makes peace in His heights, may He make peace, . . ."

For me, it was Kaddish for all the Jews in our *shtetele* who had no sons to say it for them when they were shot into the rivers, shot into the trenches, or shot and buried in the forest, unclothed and unshrouded.

Leeba drew a Mogen Dovid in the dirt over the grave, then thought better of it and erased the proof that we were there.

When will this end? We trek once again through the forest to the new location. *What will we go back to? Has Alla survived? The synagogue? Will we go back?*

Tired, I try to shut off my racing mind and focus on following the line of people ahead. They are my whole world now. I have to believe we will all survive the caves.

As we make our way between dark trunks and feathery evergreens and hard branches with spring buds on them, an owl swoops silently overhead. Later, a red fox runs beside us for a moment, before melting off into the dark. I turn back for a moment. I think the forest, with its tree branch arms and woodland creatures, is saying good-bye.

Papa makes us take our shoes and boots off when we leave the safety of the hardwood tree line and move into the rolling hills of the steppe lands. There is no cover now, as we wade through cool, misty unplowed fields and meadows and weedy pastures. He knows that barefoot, we make less noise.

He leads us to an area that dips down. Mist swirls even more heavily in the depression, ghostlike, dampening our clothes with fine droplets. The ground is cold. Our feet are cold. We put our shoes and boots back on and try not to get caught up in and torn up by the thistles and briars that cover the crevice.

We stop around a rock outcropping.

"The entrance is below," he says quietly. "You will have to wade through mud to get to it. I removed a carcass. The farmers sometimes dump their dead cattle here. So it will smell, but know the body is gone. When you get to the opening, you have to enter feet first. There are rocks like steps to take you down. Then you have to crawl forward. You can't stand for a while. I'm sending Leon in first. Light a candle when you can finally stand, Leon, so the others can follow the light. Move to the back of the area so there is room for everyone. Then I'll lead us to the grotto I've found that has room for us all."

This is hard. We look at the hole below us, yawning dark and looking like the entrance to hell on earth. No one moves, and Auntie Maya lets out one sob that sounds like a hiccup. Then she puts her fist in her mouth.

Uncle Levi says, "We can do this, Maya. For the children."
He turns to his three children, and kneels down. "This is an adventure. Maybe this is a magical cave, the cave that leads to the Land of Israel. Don't be afraid."

Leon realizes he has to start the process. He clears his throat, hands his pack to Papa, and after taking out a candle, starts the climb down. In just seconds, his head disappears and we hear sounds of sliding interrupted by impact when his foot finds a place to land. Then no sound at all.

"All right, he is in now. Let's get the women and children in next."

Mama leads the way down with Leeba and Symon. Her sister follows with Golda and Olena, and then Leon's mother lowers herself. I help the pregnant Sonia. Uncle Levi will bring Little Natan. Mr. Stadnick, Marc Rabinowitz, and Papa will be last. The men stand nervously, watchful prey scanning the horizon.

On the way down, Sonia clings to me, dragging me to the bottom of the hill as she slides in the yielding mud. My instinct is to protect her swollen belly. Luckily she is only four months pregnant, so not so big that she will have trouble fitting through the narrow opening. We slip together a few feet, clinging to each other, and I grab some nearby weeds, feeling the sharp points of nettles stab my palm.

We find footing on a boulder. Then she steps off and yelps in my ear and we are sliding again. This time, I go with it, as I see the hole just ahead, with Mrs. Stadnick's pale face sticking out. I make sure to land first so I can keep Sonia from falling on her baby. Our boots make sucking noises when we try to lift them from the mud. And a strong smell of rotting carrion lingers in the air.

"I think I'm going to vomit," Sonia whispers with urgency.

Mrs. Stadnick points to something in the dark. "I think that's Golda's shoe. She said she lost it here. Can you see if that's it?"

I reach toward the muddy lump and retrieve the wet, sticky shoe and hand it to her. Her head disappears and I kneel down first again, so I can guide Sonia, who has finished vomiting in the weeds by the hole. Feet first, I crawl back over the rock ledge into the cave entrance, feeling for a foothold. Mrs. Stadnick guides my feet down. Grateful for the help, I stop halfway down and tell Sonia to start her descent. Like this, each person guiding the foot of the next, we find our way to dry earth, the stinking weight of the bowl's mud on our shoes, boots, stockings, pants, and skirts.

A faint light filters into the rock hole and we bend toward it, starting the crawl through the rough tunnel. I follow Mrs. Stadnick's dirty boots till we emerge in a chamber of rock lit by Leon's small candle. With one hand, he guards the flickering flame from our movements when we stand.

I look around at the layers of rock that hang over and around us like soft folds of material, draped like a tent. The children look like muddy urchins. Even Leeba's braids are coated in the yellowish stuff.

There is nothing to say.

We wait for the men to follow with the packs. It takes a long time for them to get each pack through the narrow tunnel and into the lit chamber. No one says a word, not even the children. Little Natan, who is pushed in through the tunnel crying, like a reverse birth, now clings silently to his mother's skirt while he sits on the floor, his muddy thumb in his mouth, silenced by this new, stony place.

Papa lights a lantern when they are done hauling, and we begin the journey deeper into the earth's belly.

We sometimes bend over double, and walk for what seems like forever. In one cave we pass through, gray bats quiver like ivy leaves on the outer walls, and Sonia starts to scream, then cuts it off sharply by covering her mouth.

"No need," Papa calls back. "We can make all the noise we want down here. No one will hear. Scream if you need to. If it will get you through this . . . we are almost there."

I don't know how Papa found the grotto we finally step into. It's as if we are in a natural stone synagogue with vaulted ceilings. The small underground lake it houses shines green in the lamplight. It looks like a *mikveh*, a ritual bath for purification.

"Yuri told me about the water. I think he is the only person who has been down here for ages. There are some skulls in one area that look like they are from ancient times. Only a few locals know about these caves. And the old farmer who now owns this land. Hopefully he will not believe that people would hide out here. I think we are far enough in that we will be safe even if someone discovers the opening. But we still need to be careful when we exit.

"Strung after this cave are four more like this one, but without water, and beyond the final cave there is another smaller one with a stream that passes through. I suggest we use this lake for bathing and the stream cave for cooking, as there seems to be a natural vent. We can work our way through the earth to the surface and roll up some metal to make a pipe vent for cooking smoke. I'll have to go into the *shtetele* again and get some old *triniszkas* to hold up our pots. We left some in our barn. I hope they are still there. For now, let's divide the rooms per families."

The adults and Leon bending over, we walk through the four caves, which we will soon call "rooms," all about the same size, with very low ceilings and dirt floors. We take the first one, Mama's sister takes the second one, the Rabinowitzes take the third, and the Stadnicks take the fourth, with the understanding that the Cohan brothers would join them if and when they arrive. Sonia does not want to be too close to the cooking fires, and we want to give her the most privacy, so we give her and her husband a cave to themselves.

Mama looks down at the floor in our cave, slightly bent over. "I have never lived on dirt," she mutters.

Papa puts an arm around her. "This is what those Nazis make us do, huh? Live like barbarians. But the best revenge, my Eva, is just that—to *live.* . . ."

Mama nods. She heaves a big sigh and lifts her shoulders, as if shaking something off her back. She bends to pick up the shovel Papa brought. "We need to make the floor lower so we can stand better."

Papa smiles. "My practical Eva. Yes, all the rooms need to be dug up. Let's get started."

One good thing about the caves—as Papa said, we do not have to worry about making noise anymore. As the children begin to learn this, the talk gets livelier and the noise level grows. For them, it is an adventure. A new playground.

While the men begin the process of removing dirt to lower the floors, which takes about a week to complete, the children move and roll smaller cave rocks to the openings on each end of their caves. Somehow, we still feel the prairie wind blow through, even so far down, so we try to seal cracks with mud. It is a damp cold, and we soon will find out it always stays around what feels like about sixty degrees. A comfortable temperature. But to guard against hypothermia because it is still damp, we sleep close together. Partially blocking the openings helps keep our body heat in, too.

After a month, we finally have beds! It feels *so good* to get off the dirty floor. When the Cohan brothers got out safely and joined us, we had more manpower, and while Symon waited below as watch, the men snuck out at night and plundered the forest for wood and tinder. They built platforms to keep us off the cold cave dirt.

Now, Leeba and Symon and I take turns being the one who gets to sleep in the middle with a sibling on both sides to keep warm. It is comfortable under Mama's goose down coverlets, and as before, we sleep a lot. This time, for even longer hours. It's a way to conserve food and the candles and kerosene that are always running out.

Even I, who have trouble sleeping in new places, manage to close my eyes and fall into a kind of light sleep. If I don't, I open my eyes and try hard to see the curved rock ceilings above. But I can't. There is a dark that is darker than dark, and we experience it for months. We learn to dress in the pitch-black darkness, eat in it, even sew and do small tasks in it. We learn to feel our way around the tunnels that are becoming familiar. I imagine that this is what a blind person's world is like, but even they can see changes in light patterns. With no candle or kerosene wick, there is nothing.

Just unknown space.

You have to learn to trust the unknown, just ahead of you, always.

Bumps and bruises are taken for granted.

Symon whoops and hollers. Jumps up and down, loving his role. We are chasing a red fox from the front caves. It had padded down, head moving left to right, sniffing, looking for a den. It's a red fox, by the light of the candle lanterns. It bares its teeth, then backs up, as the men move forward to force it back up the entrance. It finally turns and runs. Animals are fine in the forest, moving about, but not in our home. The bats we can't control, we just stay away from their cave and their droppings. They don't hurt anyone and don't come deep into our cave rooms.

We will never know if the fox really left the caves after we turned our backs, or if it snuck in again, a shadow, and found an underground den far away from us humans.

The children play with their *motanky* dolls and with some of the gypsum crystals that come loose from their outcroppings on the ceilings and walls. The crystals are beautiful when light is shown on them. They shine clear like thick glass or cloudy diamonds or the rock candy we used to get, years ago, in the market square. But they are dangerous, too, and we have to be careful our heads don't hit them or our hands aren't cut by them when we feel around in the dark.

The children pretend the yellowish rocks are money and they buy from each other the imaginary things that they miss—books, rag dolls, colorful marbles, spinning wood dreidels, honey combs, *challah*, chocolate, plum compote for Sabbath in sweet sugary syrup. I listen, and try to remember what the food tastes like on my dry tongue.

I am beginning to forget.

There is very little that can be done in the dark. I can't even finish my *Joan of Arc*. I spend hours mindlessly tracing the raised title on the front cover, wondering what's in store for her on the next page, as she fights her battles and gets pursued.

The men get to resurface now and then for firewood and supplies and news and the exact day of the year, as Papa had to trade his watch that summer. His gold watch—for bread and *groats*.

My guesses at what day it is are usually just off by one or two days at the most.

This is when we begin to rely more and more on telling stories.

Tell me a story . . .

Pavel Cohan: "It was hard to leave the woods for the potato fields last night."

Jacob Cohan: "I've never seen such a bright moon. Like liquid silver pouring over everything."

"And something didn't feel right."

"But we waited for an hour, watching the Big Dipper move and tip across the sky, till we knew we had to move, or daylight would start to come."

"So we took our sacks into the fields and began to fill our bags with the potatoes piled in rows, dug up by the farm's workers earlier in the day. They still had the sun's warmth in them."

"We only took a handful from each pile, so it would not be obvious that many were missing, and put the wilted upper greens that were covering them back when we were done."

"Then we pushed our luck. Even though our sacks were full and the Dipper almost on its side, we had a craving for beets."

"And wild peas."

"So we went to the beet field. We found some left in the grass at the ends of the troughs. It is so late in the season, they almost were completely pushed out of the ground, just lying there for us to grab."

"We picked up a few each and put them in our pockets, when the first shot rang out."

"We didn't even look, we ran for the woods, but it seemed so far away again."

"It was. . . ."

"And the shots kept ringing out. I think there were two of them aiming at us."

"We ran, zigzagging like we have been told to do to avoid being hit."

"And we did not return directly to the caves, in case we were being followed or they had found the entrance. But it looked safe to return by morning."

"I went first, in case they were waiting, and all was clear, so now we are here, having boiled beets!"

Tell me a story . . .

Uncle Levi: "I grew up hearing tales of how my Sephardim ancestors came to Poland. We Jews have a history of searching for a promised land. In the 1400s, some of us had to flee from Spain on foot. We walked many miles to this land with fertile soil, and found a lush valley where the birds greeted us, chirping '*Po lin! Po lin!*' Which means 'lodge here.' The trees hung with pages of the Talmud, and the refugees found talmudic sayings carved into the tree bark. This told us that our ancestors had lived and studied here. There was also a cave in this valley, like our cave, called the Żydowska Szkoła, the Jewish Synagogue, by the locals. The villagers, who had protected these Jews who secretly studied their faith in the forest clearings and in the cave, believed the place to be holy. They told our people the cave had underground tunnels that led to the Land of Israel. So you see, children, we can call our cave a Żydowska Szkoła, and perhaps we will find a tunnel to that special Land."

Tell me a story . . .

Mama: "This picture is of your grandmother, your bubbe. Here she is, in her head scarf, looking so hefty and proud. Her arm is around my cousin Isaac, who died in the Holodomor, the hunger war, when he caught a fever. You see Auntie Eva, in her white dress with the high collar and embroidered shawl."

Auntie Eva: "I remember that day the photographer came to our house. Old and dusty man. Your bubbe spread her good wool rug out on the dirt patch outside and we all sat as still as we could on that hard wood bench under the eaves. She told Isaac to take his hat off. He clutched it in his hands. He loved that hat."

Mama: "And here is your bubbe in another picture a few years later. See how much weight she has lost. This is the year you were born, Leeba, 1930. We were living by then in

Kwasova, as your bubbe insisted we move across the border to Poland after Papa and I married. Stalin had by then turned the Ukrainian farms into *kolkhozes*, farms that were owned by the government, and forced the peasants by the thousands onto these farms. Many died in the struggle. Our neighbors burned their crops and slaughtered their animals in revolt. Your bubbe was right. They closed the borders two years later. We had tried to get her to come live with us, but she refused. She believed she alone was saving many of her neighbors. We tried to send food, but it was stolen along the way."

Auntie Eva: "By 1932, the peasants were starving. The state took most of the grain, even the seed grain that grew new plants. Our neighbors ate mice, bark, grass. You no longer heard dogs barking or cats mewling. They became food. Death wagons stopped by the house daily, asking if anyone was dead who needed to be taken away. My mother proudly said no each time. I love this picture of her, a burlap apron draped over her thin form while she stands in the newly turned field. Her hoe, her bucket of potatoes. She was a fine lady, your bubbe. She played Schubert expertly on the parlor piano. She painted in oils and played violin as well. But what you cannot see in this grainy photo is what is no longer in the house behind her. All sold, the piano, violin, gold jewelry, perfume bottles, on the streets to the Soviets or black marketers. She turned her great lawn into a field, and kept the two of us alive, and if she had extra, she walked to the village with a large round basket and handed out the remains to the men, women, and children begging in the streets. When she died, the government repossessed her home. A railroad employee whose son was saved by your bubbe smuggled me across the border in a box car. On the way to Poland, mothers threw starving children and babies into the open car, hoping someone at the end of the line would take them in and feed them, keep them alive at least one more day. That is how I came to Kwasova to be with you all. I comforted those I could, held two of the babies till I had to get off and leave them in the care of the older children. I hope someone took them in."

Mama: "This is a picture of your grandfather, your zeyde, in the Russian Imperial Army. See his round face and thin brows, much like Symon's. So handsome in his wool cap and epaulets, holding his sabre. He loved to sing and had a beautiful voice. . . . He died in the war. We all thought he was a brave man. But your bubbe had even more courage. It can be harder to keep a body alive than to run toward death. Remember that, children."

Tell me a story . . .

Jacob Cohan: "I found her while I was chopping wood. She crept out of the forest like a ragged wood nymph. She asked me for food. I had none, and asked who she was. She said her name was Polina, and she was the last of her family. She had managed to survive the forest raids. She came from the village east of us. She and her mother were forced to march. She escaped and made it to these woods. She lived on seeds and the underside of pine bark, slept in hollowed out beech trees. She was covered in lice and sores. She said all the forest refugees have skin diseases, at least the ones who are left. I could not leave her there. She was willing to come, but I had to carry her most of the way. I hope she can stay."

Quiet Jacob has never said so many words at once in the entire time we have known him. They came out in a rush.

And Pavel has never been so quiet.

Polina comes to us very sick. Auntie Maya immediately takes to nursing her. She removes all of the forest girl's matted clothing, cuts her hair, and bathes her with washing powder in the lake. The infested hair is taken to a faraway cave and buried, in the same way our waste is, and the clothes are boiled in the kitchen area. We can't discard them, as clothing is so hard to come by. We need every scrap, even if it is tattered and worn thin.

We've stopped wearing our boots and shoes in the caves, as they are wearing out on the rocks and gravel and Uncle Levi can no longer repair them. I am used to walking around now with cold, dirty feet, and ignore the centipedes that run about. They are harmless.

When we do laundry, we try to dry it by the cooking fires, but the cloth rarely dries entirely. So we either wear the damp clothes till they dry, or sleep with them under us, and our body heat dries the material. No one wants to sleep with Polina's clothes, so Auntie Maya washes them a second time and sleeps on them herself, while Polina lies wrapped in a quilt for two days, sleeping through most of the work hours.

"I need some beech tree leaves," Auntie Maya says to Jacob, who hovers over Polina constantly.

"I know where to go," I say eagerly, hoping to get out of the caves and see some natural light.

"No. Women are not to leave this cave," Papa says from the next cave over. "I'll go. It's been a while since I went to that tree, anyway."

Down below, we no longer have to worry about the Gestapo in the forest. We know they are there and around us and maybe even above us all the time. But so far we are safe. No one has discovered us. Now, we wait for a sign from Yuri that the Germans have left. It would be a carving of the sun, I was told. Papa does not expect to see one, but there is always hope, he says, and you have to have something to hope for.

He is right. We all hope for a round circle with rays coming from it. I draw suns in the margins of my book. Someday, maybe, I will feel those warm rays again.

Papa takes a chance that night. The moon and stars are not out for him to gauge his time away. But Polina's sores can't wait.

We always say good-bye, knowing we might never see him again. For some reason I hold him tighter than usual when my turn comes. "Bye, Papa. Say hello to Yuri's Witness Tree for me."

Mama gives him a hug.

Then Uncle Levi stations himself by the entrance and waits with an axe till Papa comes back. The men have a safe password even the rest of us don't know, which lets each one back in. If the man trying to gain entrance speaks a different password, the man on watch will know someone is with the one above, and the axe will be used in defense.

It's a summer night in late August when Papa leaves.

Legs tangled, arms askew and landing on each other in a panic. We are being roused from our dream states by someone yelling. It's pitch dark, no light to see who is standing in our cave screaming.

Then we make out names: "Pavel! Jacob! Leon!"

The voice is our uncle's.

Mama strikes a match, and we see him run past us to the other caves, with his arms and axe out in front of him to protect himself from running into a wall.

We all jump up in alarm and follow him through the dark tunnels till he gets to the last cave.

"We've been sealed in!" he keeps repeating. "We've been sealed in!"

I hear someone gag behind me, hear someone moving about. Mama's match has burned out by now, so we are feeling our way along the rough walls. Leon finally lights a bottle lantern. Some stay behind on their pallets, dazed, while the rest of us gather in the Stadnick cave, the small bit of light illuminating just Leon's figure and my uncle's.

I have never seen eyes so wide with panic as I see in that moment. Rimmed with bright white, but dark, like large limitless pools. Uncle Levi looks around him, not seeing us beyond the circle of light but knowing we are there.

"Abram did not come home this morning. I fell asleep waiting. Then woke up when I heard and then felt earth and stones raining down around me. I looked up to see a huge boulder roll over the opening. Then I heard voices, Ukrainian, and heard more rocks and dirt being shoveled. 'We know you are down there, you Jews stealing from our fields. You won't steal from us again.' I heard that, then they left.

"We are sealed in . . . ," he repeats.

Sonia starts sobbing. The children join in.

"God, why are you doing this to us?" my aunt keens, collapsing on her knees. "We have made it this far. Why this?"

Her words hang in the black air. Already, I can't feel the usual drafts that flow through the linked caves. And we have little food left, almost no kerosene and few candles. It would not be long before we would be in total darkness, starving, with not even the comfort of seeing each other's faces again.

Pavel steps into the small circle of light and faces Uncle Levi.

"We need to make another exit," he says. "There is a venting in the next room, so maybe there will be a larger vent somewhere else that we can make big enough to crawl out of."

And as quickly as we were doomed, there is a tiny bit of hope again. The men gather their sharp axes and shovels and picks. With a small amount of water in a few bottles to keep them from getting dehydrated, and with the one large thick candle we have left, they start their journey into the rest of the caves, using scratches on the walls to keep their bearings.

But the question remains, *Where is Papa?*

I guess that Mama is back on her pallet, and I feel my way to her after helping the men off. I find the arm of her wool coat, feel for her hand down the length of it, but her arm veers up. She is wiping her eyes. After she is done, her rough, damp hands feel for mine, and she covers them, quietly rubbing in warmth and comfort. I feel something wet slide into our intertwined hands, then disappear in her kneading motion.

"I forgot to blow him a kiss, Hanna. I have become so tired and forgetful," is the last thing she says into the dark.

We've lived in small spaces and in darkness for so long. We've largely grown used to it. But now it takes on a different, claustrophobic, dangerous feeling. Just knowing the exit is blocked and we're getting less air makes us suddenly aware of where we are, under tons of dirt and debris and rocks that could come crashing down on us at any moment.

Of course, the caves have survived intact for centuries, but when you are lying in the dark, with tons of rock over your head, it presses down on your chest and makes your heart beat fast. Auntie Maya has the hardest time, starts breathing rapidly and crying out that she is having heart distress. Which makes Little Natan and Golda start crying. Soon, the caves are filled with wails and words of comfort from Mama and Sonia.

Leeba and I hold hands in bed till the crying subsides, and we hear Mama's tired, dragging feet make their way to her empty pallet.

The walls seem to contract and expand, like a living body. I hear my heartbeat in my ears. I feel my blood whooshing around in my veins.

I get up and join her, to keep her warm and fill the empty spot. She holds me close and rocks.

I can't tell if she is rocking me—or herself—to sleep.

Tell me a story . . .

Polina: "My father and brother were taken into service for the Russian army. My mother and I were left to fend for ourselves. My mother is . . . was, very beautiful. When the Germans came, they made us wear armbands that we had to make and sew ourselves. A white background and a blue Jewish star. Every day my mother went to their camp to serve them. She left clean, and groomed. She came home with messy hair, scratches on her face, tears in her clothing that she would mend before bedtime. I did not dare to ask.

"She would not let me leave the house or answer the door. She kept me hidden in a closet when the Germans came to visit and drink with their guns at their sides. She told me to recite the first line of the Shema if I ever heard one of her guests open my closet door, so I would not die alone, so I would be part of all the Jews who had come before and who would come after, for surely I would be shot on sight.

"She heard talk over a meal one day that the village was to be declared *Judenfrei*. That all Jews should pack a bag and appear in the town square the next day. One officer told her not to worry, that he would find a way to make her invisible, so he could keep her. But she could not leave me and he would not take me, too.

"What do you pack when you know you are going nowhere? My mother had heard enough rumors to know where we were headed. Still, you pack with hope and remembrance. Some fresh clothes, some jewelry for possible bribes, a prayer shawl, a festival prayer book, a few photos. You close that satchel, and tell yourself it is only the material. It is not you.

"We gathered in the market square. Fancy clothes. Ragged clothes. It was very quiet. Then the trucks appeared and we were told to fall in line behind them. My mother knew we were not headed to the promised Janowska labor camp. That this was an impossible journey.

"They took pictures of us, while we marched. And laughed...

"On the second day, she saw a chance. She took my satchel, and without a word of good-bye or a last endearment she pushed me with all her might into the roadside bushes. I know those behind us saw. But I was not betrayed. They kept marching. I could feel their hope that one of us might survive and tell their story someday. Finally the truck in the rear passed by and out of sight. The silence, after the constant sound of shuffling, defeated feet and of children whimpering, was... deafening.

"I fled into the woods. I met other Jews in hiding, with nothing to share and often near death. I tried to survive on my own. I could not. One cold night I crawled into a tree hole to die. That is when I heard Jacob pass by. I crawled out, and he found me. *Danken Got!* Thank God!"

Sonia's husband, Marc, comes back, while we pick at some stale bread. He's been searching for a possible exit for several days now. He lights a bottle lantern, just briefly, so we can see his face, which has a gentle, tired smile on it. His heavy black brows and dark hair look gray in the light, and then I realize he is covered in dirt.

"They found an area that is close to the surface and are making good headway. Though I wish we had a *shamir*, King Solomon's magic worm, to do the stone cutting. We should have another exit soon. We'll make sure to keep that covered. We will not try to open up the one they sealed. We want them to think we are . . . stuck down here."

"But how will Papa get back in?" Symon cries out.

He pauses. "I don't know. I guess we will have to send someone out to try and find where he is."

"I know where to go." I stand up.

"You?" His brows slant down and he looks at me over the bridge of his nose.

"Yes, to the tree." I look at Mama, and her forehead is squinted in confusion. "I call it Yuri's Witness Tree. It's the one he and Yuri leave messages to each other on. Like the talmudic sayings carved into the trees in Uncle Levi's legend. If Papa wanted to leave us a message, he would leave one there. Also, it's a beech tree. . . ."

We all look at Polina, wrapped and quiet in her quilt. Her sores are getting very infected, and it is only a matter of time before the infection rages in her blood.

"Well, nothing can be done anyway until the exit is completely ready. We will discuss this when the rest get back. I'm staying here for now so someone is with you," Marc states firmly.

There is nothing worse than waiting for something to happen when two lives are on the line. I pace back and forth, planning how I will get back to the tree, trying to see in my mind the path in the moonlight.

But what if there is no moonlight? Things are too urgent to wait. I have to make the trip in either case, light or no light.

When the men come back, dusty and exhausted but relieved to have found an exit, they argue in the dark over me going out. Eventually they all agree that Uncle Levi will go with me.

"But Papa felt it would be best if I went to the tree alone," I try, "because he thought I might survive if I were caught. They will shoot Uncle Levi."

"We have no guns to fight them with, but you need someone with you who has learned how to move about quietly at night and be a second eye and ear for you. You have no choice in the matter, Hanna," Uncle Levi says firmly.

I bite my lip and nod, even if they can't see me. At least they are letting me go.

Mama gets me ready, allowing me to wear my boots. She blackens my face and hands with soot. My hair is now below my shoulders, so she braids it and covers it with a dark scarf to keep the braids from snagging and leaving a trail of hair for a well-trained hunter or soldier to find.

When Leeba hugs me good-bye, she says, "Find Papa."

When Mama hugs me good-bye, she says nothing, but I feel like my ribs could crack for a breathless moment.

Symon holds my hand to the new exit.

Leon holds both my shoulders in the dim light from the hole above and looks into my eyes. "I told them I would take you, but they would not let me." I look down from his intense green gaze, embarrassed. "*Hazak ve-amatz.* Be strong and have courage." He lightly kisses my forehead.

I feel scorched where his lips touched my soot-blackened skin.

They show me where to place my hands and feet. I crawl up the rock wall to the sliver of light overhead. I make it to the top and poke my head through the hole and into my first look at the real world in ten months. And inhale my first breath of fresh air. I had forgotten how sweet meadow air is in late summer. How silky smooth.

The moon and stars are not out. We have no sky clock to guide us. We will have to get to the tree and make our way back quickly in order to beat the sunrise.

We both carry knives in case we are separated. My hand curls around the hard shaft. The knife steadies me.

Walking through the dark meadow is easy. We have no obstructions and there's a dark visual point in the tree line to the woods just a few hundred yards away, but it still feels like miles as we push through the sea of tall June meadow grass that blooms with wheatlike stalks on the ends. Uncle Levi walks behind me, figuring it is the best way he can protect me, as then he would be able to pounce forward. I think of the two young saboteurs we had tried to save, many months ago, their brave little backs disappearing into the fields at night.

If those little boys could be brave, so could I.

As we walk, I think about how our homes shape us. How wood and stone and brick and the dimensions of space and angles and rooflines and all those qualities that go into a shelter mold our impressions and interactions with our surroundings. In the *shtetele*, I was used to the limitless feeling of the lanes and paths and roads that took us in soft rises to our daily stops. I'd lived under a pitched roof that made me aware of space in a way that was so different from the cabin with the high vaulted ceiling and strict confines of a square space. In the caves, space is compacted, unseen boundaries in the dark that could trip you up or hurt your head if you weren't careful. Small, hard, rough spaces carved into the earth that make you feel primitive and isolated.

Now, in the dark, but outside in the vast meadows of the forest-steppe, heading to the dense woods, I feel a sense of freedom I haven't felt in months. *This is how life should be, being able to move freely about in space with no chains or fears or limits.*

Occasionally Uncle Levi stops me for a moment, resting his hand on my shoulder. Or he makes me aware of a twig or rock that could be stepped on or dislodged, giving us away.

We pass the same copse of birches twice before I realize I've taken a wrong turn. I change course and head to the right and up the hill instead of to the left.

That's when I hear a sound like a small barking dog. We are nearing the owls' winter roosting place, which means the beech is nearby. Even in summer, an owl is keeping watch.

I pick my way through brambles and thickets to a clearing, in the middle of which is Yuri's Witness Tree. Wings almost brush my head. A feather wafts to the ground. I take it as a welcome, and pick up the downy gift and put it in my pocket.

Then I run eagerly to the trunk. The writing side is in front of me this time. My heart beats faster as I get close, seeing a new carving. When I reach the mossy ground that meets the surfacing roots at the base of the tree, I run my hand over newly cut bark. It's a single, large line.

"What is it?"

"It's from Papa," I say with confidence. "He's telling me—us—he's alive."

"But where is he?"

"I don't know, somewhere in these woods is my guess. He's been hoping I would make it back here to see this. Only he would put this here, and only I would know it was him."

"So what do we do now?"

"I have to leave him a message, let him know we are alive and can get in and out of the cave, that there is a new entrance."

That makes sense, but how? What secret symbol can I put on the tree to let him know all that important information? What can be left that will not tip off the Germans?

Letting him know we are alive is the easy part. With my knife, I make sixteen scratches into the bark, then remember Polina and add another for seventeen in total. That will show him it is me leaving the marks, not Yuri, and that we are all safe. But how do we let him know about the new exit?

Uncle Levi is stroking his beard. He is not my father's brother, but still, in the dark, he has that same gesture, and it makes my heart ache. How can I get my father back to us?

"He can only find the new entrance with some sort of marking, but what can we put out that our Ukrainian neighbors won't spot? A stick?"

"I can't draw a stick and make it look like something besides another mark." I think of Alla. All her natural symbols and what they mean, and what I could replicate with a knife. A few more owl barks from the branches above.

And that is when I know that I am not alone. I don't have a name for it yet, but something like a fire starts inside my belly as a dawning of something that is beyond my understanding grows in intensity and spreads throughout my arms to my hands.

I reach down and pull out the feather.

Uncle nods. I put it back in my *kurtka* pocket and carve the image of an owl feather under the count marks. Then a partial circle below the feather's quill, to signal it will be near a hole. My uncle makes some low whistling noises, his own signal, but no answer comes. Papa is not within ear shot.

He gives me a lift with his cupped hands. I pull myself up to a low hanging branch, sit on it, and cut down some smaller branches, which he then strips of leaves. The leaves he stuffs in his *kurtka* pockets.

Just as I swing down, the moon finally comes out from behind the clouds. It is far to the west, and the Big Dipper is almost horizontal. We have to leave now as sunrise is nearing. Uncle Levi grabs me around the waist, lets me down on the ground, then takes my arm as we descend the hill to return to the meadow.

"What's that?" He stops short. I run into him.

We pause, our ears straining to catch what he'd heard. There it is, something like a popping noise in rapid succession. We look at each other's soot-covered faces in alarm, wide eyes shining white. Gunfire, probably from the submachine guns the Germans now carry. They are the only arms in the area that can fire rapidly, Leon had told me. The upgraded MP-43 is one reason the Germans have such a big advantage over the Red Army and any resistance.

Tac-tac-tac-tac. The popping sounds come again from our left, up at the top of the hill.

"We have to separate," I whisper to him.

"No!"

"Yes, Papa warned me about this. If they find us together, they will for sure kill us. But if they only find me, we both stand a chance."

Uncle Levi shakes his head, but he reaches into his *kurtka* and takes out some leaves and rams them in my pockets.

"My sweet niece, your father may have been right last year, but not now . . . that's why I came with you. We have not passed along to you womenfolk how bad things have gotten. We need to go quickly now, *together*. And if I push you ahead and stay behind, *keep running*."

These last instructions he pants out while we run as quietly as we can through the brush, trying not to snap twigs and branches, hoping we sound like deer moving through: "Don't look back. But don't . . . run to the caves . . . run to the edge . . . of the woods . . . find a place . . . to hide . . . till it's safe . . . to reenter."

But it is impossible at that speed not to make some noise.

And soon, shouts of *"Schnell! Schnell!"*

The crashing sounds of pursuit.

Then the moment my uncle gives me a huge push.

I fall forward into dirt and leaves, my hands breaking my fall, my wrists bending backward in pain.

I can't run away. I turn in the brush, on the ground, and watch his figure retreat and then run off to the right, making a great commotion, leading them away from me.

"No!" I cry to myself. "God, don't do this!"

Then the dark shape of many pursuers . . . the serpent unchained.

Insects crawl and whirl around all night, grasshoppers, mole crickets, flies. But the heart beating in my chest is louder than all the chirps and saw noises their wings make. I am flat on the ground, my ear to the earth, listening for vibrations, feet coming near. Mosquitoes buzz and bite. Everywhere. I don't dare slap them dead.

A beautiful white moth, with black markings, settles on the glint of my knife blade, which I clutch. If it can see the light, the SS can, too. I knock the moth off gently and put the knife under my body.

The sun is at its highest point over the meadow when I dare to crawl through the grass to the new exit hole. I don't know exactly where it is, but find small signs of our night journey and follow them back to the hole. Then I realize I don't know the safe password. We'd expected my uncle to be with me. So I just push aside the camouflage brush and board and speak into the dark below.

"It's me, Hanna. I'm alone."

I stay low, afraid of bullets grazing me from behind.

I put a leg into the hole and feel for a foothold, and then someone is guiding me carefully down. It is Leon with a huge smile on his face, the dimple prominent, till he sees I really *am* alone. I fall into his arms and weep for the first time since I'd been forced to abandon Uncle Levi.

I've never felt pain so fierce. It is one thing to have a father disappear and wonder, and another to see a relative run away to save you, with the SS in pursuit. To know that someone might be alive, if not for you. I do not want to face my aunt or my little cousins. I tell Leon what happened, and he gently unknots the scarf and strokes my hair to calm me, then makes an attempt to wipe the soot off my face with the cloth.

"I'll tell your aunt," he says softly. "They are all sleeping now, in any case. Why don't we wait here to give them some more sleep, more time before knowing this. I'll get you some water and food."

Some light filters down from above, and I sit in the dirt where the moat of swirling dust shines on me. The leaves in my coat were the only thing that kept me moving forward and back to the caves. Someone needed me at both ends, but one I knew I could help, the other . . .

I see the glow from his bottle lantern before I see Leon. He blows it out to save the wick and brings with him a tin cup of water and some dried blackberries. I gulp them all down and drain the cup of the cool water.

We wait a few hours for the others to sleep. Our time is spent in silence or in talking about the feather carving and the tree. I can't talk about my uncle. Or the SS. I can't look at Leon.

"How long can we do this for?" I ask him, looking at the ground.

"What? Stay down here?"

"Yes, how long do you think you can stay down here and stay . . . normal?"

He is quiet for so long, I decide he is not going to answer. Then, "I can stay down here forever if I have to. All the people I care for most are here." He glances sideways. "How can you or me or anyone live through this and be the same again? We know too much of what evil can be and what real, intense fear is. It changes you."

I chew on that for a while.

He continues, "But maybe some of the change is for the better, if we can get through all this and remain whole. Maybe we will be better people for it."

"I wonder how Alla is doing."

"Alla?"

"Mrs. Petrovich. She is so alone, but I guess she has her chickens and our dog to keep her company, if the SS haven't taken them away yet."

"Oh, your neighbor. I think she is still there, but if we can ever make it back to the *shtetele*, I'll look in on her. She is far enough away from the market square. I think we can do that safely."

"Thank you."

More silence for a long time, while I relax slightly. Leon's concerned presence starts to settle my heartbeat. It has not stopped racing since the pursuit. I feel a bit sick now. And have a headache.

When it is time to go to the others, he stands and holds his hand out to help me up. I take it, warming at the touch, but am too tired and anxious to register anything more. It is just the hand of a gentle being at that moment.

I clutch it for support.

Auntie Maya sits like a white ghost on her pallet. I want to crawl in a hole and bury myself to avoid the expression on her face, one of utter loss. While on the other hand, my mother has to fight to hide her joy. The two sisters, each with very different news. Mama sits next to my aunt and holds her hand, as I had once held hers.

It is troubling that Auntie Maya, the one amongst us who is always crying out or being hysterical, is quiet now. Her stony silence is worse than any wailing could have been. She looks almost frozen.

It isn't until Polina lifts her head from the ground and calls to her, too weak to rise, that Auntie Maya focuses back on the present. She stands. She slowly walks. Over to the girl she has basically adopted.

"*I* made it," Polina whispers. "I got away from them. Maybe he did, too. There are many places to hide in those woods. . . ."

I see what she is doing. Just as Auntie Maya begins preparations with the beech leaves to make poultices for Polina's sores, Polina is trying to cover up my aunt's emotional sores by giving her that one essential thing we all need for survival—hope.

She even gave a glimmer to me.

Tell me a story . . .

The children want to hear my story, the story of what happened the night I went to Yuri's Witness Tree (we haven't yet let the youngest children know that their father is gone now, too). But I cannot tell the story, even if I leave that part out. I roll over in bed and ignore them. Leeba makes shushing noises and tells them to go away, then strokes my head like a little mother. Mama fills the silence in by telling another fairytale with a happy ending.

But I can't sleep. Images of my uncle and dark shadows in pursuit won't stop running through my mind after everyone else goes to bed. I finally get off the pallet and feel for a shawl, then make my way to the underground lake. When the dirt starts to slope, I sit down. There is nothing to see in that cave darkness. Just blackness. But you can sense the open expanse of water before you. I dip my bare feet into the edge, where the water meets the sandy dirt, knowing I'm sending out ripples that I'm unable to watch expand.

What is expanding outside of the safety of our underground caves? What ripples, or torrents, are being set off by the German army and their evil leader that will expand ever outward and forward from our lives and into others' in the future?

I want to have that feeling again that I'd felt in the forest, when I heard the Long-eared owl bark its presence, letting me know I wasn't alone and that something or someone greater was watching out for me.

I wait for that glowing inside, but nothing comes. Maybe it can't reach me so deep under the crust of dirt and grassy meadows.

Before we go to bed, Mama sews the owl feather to a wide branch on a thistle bush near the entrance for Papa to find. She tells us, after we climb onto our pallets, that she'd sewn every bit of love she has for him into the minute, solid stitches that she promises us will go unseen to the naked eye.

I try to send out thoughts and prayers, like water ripples, like a beacon, to bring him back. To make that feather wave and glow in the dark. But I worry that the ancient bedrock overhead is just too thick.

Sonia gives birth to a baby girl in September 1943. The caves echo with her animal moans for hours. I hold my hands over my ears. *This is birth?* I think. *Who would want this?*

"Come here, Hanna," Mama calls to me when it quiets down. "It's a girl!"

I hear relief in her voice. She and Auntie Maya have prayed for this. It's harder on Jewish boys who have to be circumcised, and who might be ordered to drop their pants to prove they are not Jewish when discovered by the Gestapo. We heard this was what they did to Osip the Butcher. Right in the streets of Kwasova. He'd been ordered to drop his pants in front of his neighbors.

I make my way with Mama through darkness till we come upon Sonia and her new baby in her arms, on the ground, bathed in a bit of light from a bottle candle. Sonia's straight brown hair is greasy and dark against her forehead, but her cheeks are brilliant in the soft yellow glow. She looks happy for the first time since I met her.

It is the prettiest baby I have ever seen, lying on her bare chest. Even prettier than Leeba had been. A perfect little person. With a bit of damp fuzzy dark hair on her head and with light blue eyes and long lashes. Such pale skin, though. I see thin, purple, spidery veins mapped around her little skull.

I take a finger and stroke her soft, wrinkled shoulder. Her shoulder is also covered in downy hair, which I know, from the birth of Leeba and Symon, will soon fall off.

Sonia smiles drowsily up at me, while the older women murmur *tkhines,* childbirth prayers.

"Her name is Arashel. It means 'strong and protected,'" she says tiredly. "You'll have one of your own someday."

Will I? I wonder. Will I grow old enough to marry, and be in a world where I would *want* to have a baby? It's hard to imagine, from this great distance underground, where we are being made to live like lowly voles.

After Sonia recovers, the older women take her to the lake, our temporary *mikveh,* and immerse her in the green water. I can tell they feel some comfort in this ancient re-birth ceremony. It belongs to them, this purification ritual— to us—and on this day, we lay claim to it with pride and tenderness.

We know it's around mid-September, so that means Leon has made it to seventeen. We have nothing material to give him. I have nothing to give him, as I'd hoped I would. But we still celebrate. We sing to him, clap to keep away evil spirits and honor him.

Later, I light a candle and go out looking for Leon. I find him alone, by the lake, and sit next to him. He looks sad.

"You should be happy," I say. "You weren't sure you would see this day. If it is the exact right day." I try a joke.

He throws a pebble far out into the water. We hear it *plop.*

"Now I can't help but wonder if I will see eighteen . . . twenty. Have a family." He turns to me. Candlelight dances across his face. His eyes are dark and I can't see the expression in them. "Kiss a woman, even."

I gulp.

And summoning all my courage, I lean forward and give him the one thing I can give him on his birthday, the one thing I *want* to give him.

At first his head snaps back, shocked, then he leans back in. His lips are dry and cracked. So are mine. His scruffy beard tickles my chin. It's not a romantic kiss, not the way I'd dreamed about kissing him, not the place I'd pictured it happening. But it is the first time our lips have touched other lips in this way, and it feels special. I can feel his breathing change. Faster.

We pull away and look back at the lake, too embarrassed to look at each other, but I hear a grin in his voice when he says, "We'd better keep this birthday present to ourselves." And, "Thank you, sweet, brave Hanna."

With the SS so close by, even at night the men don't dare to stick their heads above ground to look out for Papa or wave to alert him, in case he is watching. (Mama had pulled the nettle branch into the hole to sew on the feather.) The best they can do is to stay on constant watch below the exit hole, so they can listen for him if he starts rooting around. We can't afford to lose another man.

We busy ourselves to avoid thinking about the two missing fathers.

Auntie Maya throws herself into nursing Polina back to health, and decides she should teach me, as the eldest in the next generation, how to boil the beech leaves, cool them, and apply them like a poultice.

It isn't easy to witness such infection. I've never seen open sores. They look like her pink insides are exposed, oozing and angry. One is on the inside of her right thigh, and I blush to see the triangle of hair that barely covers her mound. She has to spread her thighs to allow us to work between them. I try to concentrate on the sore, and Polina turns her head and closes her eyes tightly as I apply the poultice.

I understand in that moment the intense vulnerability of the body as victim. How we as humans need other humans we can trust to take care of our bodies and souls sometimes. How we have to put ourselves into a vulnerable position for help. And how we have to pray that those around us have empathy.

How can the Germans not see our suffering? I think to myself, as I boil a new batch of leaves. *How can they hurt people like Polina? Babies? What makes them so cut off from their humanity?*

There will always be murderers amongst us, but a whole country? Against a whole group of people? I can't fathom it. The understanding of it all seems as unreachable as the moon and sun above.

Because I'm in the kitchen, boiling water over a fire to do laundry, I am the first one, besides Pavel who has been on watch, to know something is happening. I hear sounds I've never heard before coming from the tunnels beyond. Like dogs barking.

But it can't be the owls?

Then I realize, as the sounds grow closer, that it's Pavel emitting some sort of Yiddish war cry. I freeze. Have the Germans found the caves?

I prepare to turn over the boiling pot if I need to stop someone from entering. I put my hands on the hot edge, and . . .

A lantern light, more whooping, and there is Pavel jumping up and down along the tunnel to the kitchen.

"He's back! Your father came back!"

And there, behind Pavel, is Papa's mud-streaked face, smiling sheepishly at the loud escort. I drop my wood spoon and run into his dusty arms.

Pavel continues calling and everyone comes rushing toward us. I know I have to move aside to let Mama in, but I don't want to let go. Somehow, he holds us all—me, Leeba, Symon, Olena, Golda, and Mama.

We are all one big cluster of joy and relief.

Papa returns with a sack full of mealy corn with damp husks, the last of the summer harvest, and fresh beans that he'd found growing between the corn rows in the field. We haven't had fresh food in weeks. He also got a bit of sourdough from a peasant who had hidden him, in exchange for the fake wood rifle he'd carried and the beech leaves he'd gathered and been unable to bring to us. He also holds a handful of wilted daisies for Mama, the first flowers she's seen since we fled to the cave.

We boil the beans and some of the corn; the rest of the cobs we hang to dry to be ground into cornmeal later. Mrs. Stadnick kneads the sourdough with a bit of flour and bakes it on a metal sheet to make *pletzlach*. That night, we feast. The corn is starchy but almost as sweet as sugar, and the beans need no salt or butter, which we don't have, anyhow. With a few bites of the *pletzlach*, it's possible to feel almost full, a sensation we're not used to anymore. We all rub our bellies with glee.

The food brings unusual color to our faces and a brightness to our eyes. We celebrate with a few bottle lanterns on the ground, so we can see the returned and witness everyone's happiness in the circle we make up in Auntie Maya's large cave. Her eyes are the only ones that remain strained, and she hangs back, not saying anything. I watch as she forces herself to eat, picking at the food and putting it in her mouth, chewing mechanically, swallowing with effort.

Papa is famished, and we have to let him eat first. Then we wait for his story.

Papa: "I had the leaves and was returning to the caves when I heard the commotion. Voices, calling back and forth. So I stopped, hid, and watched a group moving across the meadow from the direction of the farm. They had shovels, and knew where to go. It was with horror that I saw them stop at our entrance, then slide down the ravine. I knew what they were doing. One of them must have seen us in their potato fields and followed us back to the caves one night. Probably a hunter, because only a hunter would know how to be more silent than we are.

"I had my fake gun. But what could I do? One against five, with shovels and anger in their hearts. Even our farmers are turning against us. They see us as thieves. We take so little, but they just see the taking, and the Germans have poisoned even them against us. Our neighbors have forgotten the words of Deuteronomy, words we both share: 'When you reap the harvest in your field and overlook a sheaf in the field, do not turn back to get it; it shall go to the stranger, the fatherless, and the widow.'

"I waited until they left, then waited some more, then made my way to the ravine and found the entrance impassible. I could not move the largest boulder, and I knew you were trapped inside. In the meantime, the SS were doing more sweeps of the woods, and this time at night, with the help of some Ukrainian locals. They are getting wise to our habits. In any case, I had to find some sort of shelter. I headed back to our forest cabin and discovered others living there. I peered in the little window. In the candlelight, I did not know them, so I did not trust them. I went back to the safety of the brush and found a hollow tree to shelter in. Like Polina."

He smiles at her, her head in Jacob's lap as she listens and nods.

"I felt helpless, not knowing what to do. I stayed in the tree for a long time, thinking. Then I returned to carve one long mark into our tree. I wanted you all to know I was alive at that point in time, that I was in those woods, on the slim chance one of you got out and came back. I checked it every night for a message in return.

"But one night, after I checked the tree, I heard shouts back at the cabin. I wanted to get to the safety of my hollow tree, but could not chance getting too close to the commotion. So I climbed another sturdy tree nearby. I could see our cabin. The shouts were from SS and Ukrainians, who marched everyone outside. I still did not recognize the people hiding out. The SS shot them . . . all."

The word *all* is so heavy on his lips. I know this means there were women and children.

"The SS had chicken wire wrapped around their gray helmets, with branches and leaves woven in for camouflage. The Ukrainians also wore camouflage. They pulled out cigarettes and smoked, standing and talking and laughing over the bodies." He stops for a few moments. "I was watching with the owls. One man was not dead. He rose and ran, and they followed in pursuit."

I remember seeing them chasing someone that night in the distance, and then hearing shots. So even that man had not gone far. But Papa does not know they were chasing his brother-in-law as well. We hadn't wanted to spoil his homecoming right away. He assumed Uncle Levi was out scavenging.

"They were gone all night. I stayed in the tree. Early in the morning, when the dew was still rising, they returned with shovels. The Ukrainians removed all the clothing and jewelry, and buried the bodies, right in the clearing by our old cabin. Then there was an argument over the wedding bands. The SS pointed their guns at the Ukrainians and forced them to turn the gold over. They all left in the afternoon. When it was dark, I climbed down and stood over the spot and said Kaddish."

We are quiet for a time, letting the moment pay further tribute.

Then he gives me a slight smile. "I made my way to our tree, to see if there was any answer to my message. My smart girl not only came and found mine, but left me a message in return that I could understand. I knew then that you had found a way out, and that somehow a feather would lead me to the way back in. The whole world opened back up for me again, and gave me purpose."

I look at Auntie Maya. Her eyes hollow, surrounded by her children. *It's time*, I thought. *It's my responsibility*. I step forward, my hands shaking.

"Papa . . ." He looks surprised at being interrupted.

"Papa, I didn't mean to leave him behind, but he pushed me. Uncle Levi . . ." Mama puts her hand on my shoulder. "Those men heard us running away and came after us with their guns. Uncle Levi saved my life. He pushed me down and ran off to distract them so I could get away."

Papa shakes his head, as if denying the news, and looks at Auntie Maya with deep sadness and a question in his eyes.

"We don't know where he is," Mama adds gently. "He has not returned."

"I do not know what happened to Levi. I did not see him that night, or any other. I made my way to a peasant's barn, a man who had helped me before, and he hid me in the loft for a few weeks. The SS were still searching nearby. When they left, and I was free to go, I asked to trade the leaves and anything else I had on me for some food. He took my knife and our fake gun and gave me the sourdough, saying that was all he had, but that I could help myself to some corn in the fields. He gave me a flour sack. So that is how we are dining tonight, by the goodness of this man's heart, and by the cleverness of a girl who knows how to communicate without words. I found the feather glowing in the moonlight, waving to me from a field of grass."

If a grin can be sad, his is.

"*Yidishn kop*," Mama murmurs, tugging at his salt-and-pepper beard. He catches her hand and kisses it.

I glow, too, for a moment. I'd done something right and helped bring Papa home. But it's hard not to think about the fact that one of us is still missing.

Papa goes to Auntie Maya, who has listened silently all along. He kneels in front of her, takes her hands. "Levi saved my daughter. We will honor him and pray for his safe return tonight." Then we turn to the children and talk to them and give as much comfort as we can, now that they have found out that their father has disappeared.

There is urgency to our nights after that one. The SS won't give up looking for Jews and partisans, and it is getting more dangerous to leave the caves. I make a large scarecrow out of long meadow grass, bunched together to make arms and a neck. Symon calls him the *Tzeler*. He is still bitter about his friend and feels that if it gets shot at, it should have the name of someone who deserves to be shot. Papa says Symon has to work out his own feelings of anger. So the *Tzeler*, it is.

One of the Cohan's knit caps is put over the grass head. The men stick the *Tzeler* out the entrance hole, to see if it will get shot at, before they exit. And the men begin to draw lots to be the first one to climb out, just in case a shot comes late. It is harvest time, and we have to gather what we can before winter. But we can't plunder the nearby fields anymore as they are being watched by the men who'd sealed us in. Instead, the men take chances and venture farther away from the caves. Only two go at a time now, as we can't afford to lose them all at once. They carry sharpened picks, crow bars, and axes for protection.

In between small deliveries of apples, winter pears, sugar beets, carrots, corn, beans, cabbage, and potatoes, they bargain with the last of our money and spare clothing for candles, kerosene, washing soap (which is almost nonexistent now), flour, matches, a few precious pinches of salt, and news of Levi Yurkovich.

It is the quiet Cohan brother, Jacob, who finally comes back to the caves with a slender string of a rumor. His attachment to Polina has grown, and the two often sit together as she improves, while he recites to her the poetry of the famous Ukrainian Taras Shevchenko. One day she said she missed the taste of eggs. This gave Jacob a mission, and against all advice, he snuck into the *shtetele*, alone. Even Pavel won't go back there, as it is fully occupied by the SS, who have new orders, from Gestapo Chief Koelner who had passed through Kwasova on Sukkōt, to shoot all Jews on sight.

But Jacob made it to Alla's and back. It is, in fact, the last trip any of us will make outside the caves. He dumps his rucksack on the dirt, heavy with success.

"There are new bandit fighting troops, with orders from Hitler to continue sweeping the woods, mountains, and marshes, even the meadows, for bunkers hiding Jews and partisan rebels," he informs us.

"What if those peasants who sealed us in tell them of the Jews who steal from their fields and live below the meadow? And then lead them to the ravine entrance?" Marc Rabinowitz asks.

"At least we left it sealed," Papa says. "They might think we perished."

"This bandit group is professional. I think we should seal up the second entrance and stay below ground," Jacob advises. "I don't know how even I survived this last trip. There are soldiers stationed at all crossroads and patrolling at all hours. It is time to stay put till the Russians can take the land back."

The idea is frightening, to stay below, sealed in like avalanche victims once again. But it is decided, with Jacob returning against all odds, to seal up the second entrance for the winter. No one would leave again till spring. We who had stayed below could not hear the approaching gunfire nor see the night sky light up from mortar fire, but the men who'd recently left the caves saw and heard and knew that the Russians were trying to take back the country, but so far, were unable to break through the German line of defense.

Jacob's sack of contraband is therefore highly prized, but not more so than his information on Uncle Levi.

"Mrs. Petrovich let me in her back door when I said I was a friend of the Slivka family. She had finished her supper of dry bread and cheese but let me have some of what was left over while she boiled eggs for Polina. She sat across from me and told me there was a rumor in town, which she had heard from Mrs. Davydenko. She said her husband, Chief Davydenko, saw a man in ragged clothing digging in your yard late at night, but he ran away when her husband confronted him.

"She doesn't know if it was Levi, I'm sorry," he says gently to Auntie Maya.

"But he may be alive!" she cries, looking happier. "That's all I need to know for now. Who else would know where to dig?"

"Your dog is a bit skinnier, but happy," Jacob jokes to Symon, who still looks sad, thinking about Ovid. "She said she pretended to be blind when soldiers came knocking on her door, looking to take food and animals. She gave them her carved wood chest so they would not take away the last of her prize hens. They left Ovid, thinking she needed the dog to see for her.

"And I was given this special gift to deliver to Hanna." Jacob reaches into a pocket and takes out a ragged handkerchief. He puts it in his palm and uses his other hand to lift the folds.

I gasp when he reveals an ornately decorated *pysanka*.

"She said she made it for you for your fifteenth birthday and always hoped she would be able to give it you in person, but that this is the next best thing, knowing you are alive and will hold it."

I look at Papa and Mama. My eyes must be begging enough. They look at each other, then both nod at me.

The blown egg is one of the most beautiful *pysanky* Alla has ever made. Knowing her belief in the symbols of nature, I "read" my egg's message. On one side she'd painted a green tree with wide-ranging branches. It looks like Yuri's Witness Tree, but I know she means it to be the Tree of Life. Green for the victory of life over death. Alla is telling me to try to be strong, no matter what I am facing. I smile to see a brown background. No longer white for innocence, but not black either, as I still have a life to be filled out. Around the tree are the outlines of beige oak leaves, which symbolize strength. She wants me to be strong. Under the tree is a brown deer with antlers, which is a wish for food for a whole year.

The back has the most colorful bird I've ever seen. Its head, partially in clouds, is bright blue and looks like an eagle's head with peacock feathers sprouting out the top; the green and purple ornate wings, spreading across the span of the egg's width, are rimmed in orange fire. The huge yellow talons seem to be emerging from blue roiling waves. Around the bird she'd etched yellowish wheat flowers, for health.

I hold this talisman, proof of goodness, in my hand, and cry. I cry as I haven't cried since we left home. I weep and wail without shame till my cries echo in the hollow chamber, which feel like a dark prison now.

I want my life back, my home, my Alla.

Leeba and Mama hold me because I'm too weak to stand. I want to crawl back home, out of this dirty dark hole in the ground. If crying is a form of breathing, as Papa says, then I am breathing out all that is hidden deep down inside me, things I didn't even know were there.

I want to gather flowers, climb trees and pick the fruit from them, the skin warm from the sun, taste the sweet juices, and the sun ... how I miss the feel of its brightness burning my skin, warming me inside to the excitement of a summer day with nothing to do but live and move freely about under the great blue sky. Life had even been better in the forest, with fresh evergreen and pine smells and bird song and light between cracks and the feeling of space beyond the mossy walls.

They put me to bed early. Mama stays with me in the dark and strokes my head till I fall asleep, the egg gently clutched in my hand.

Papa examines the egg the next day, by the brief light of a precious match. I hold my breath, waiting for his disapproval, until the match fizzes out. The smell of sulfur hangs between us.

"Your friend Alla honored our beliefs with this image of the large bird. I cannot tell if it is a phoenix, or the Ziz." His words come out of the darkness, heavy and solemn.

"The phoenix is a special bird in the Talmud. Noah's son Shem tells of an encounter with the bird on the ark by his father: the bird has abstained from eating in order to not bother his protectors. Because of this, Noah blesses the bird with eternal life. In this story, patience and self-sacrifice are the virtues."

I see all of us, lying in the dark on a surging deck, waiting.

"Or, it could be the Ziz. Biblical creatures include Leviathan, who rules the waters, and Behemoth, who rules the land. Ziz rules the skies. She is so large, her feet stand in deep waters, her head reaches into the clouds, and her large wings, when they spread, block the sun and protect the earth from the wind, which could destroy the earth. Some say her head rises so high, she sings to God.

"I do not know which bird Alla painted for you, or what she is trying to say. Perhaps both. Have patience, and be protected."

His large hand is on mine, placing the egg back carefully in the cradle of my palm.

Alla finally found a bridge.

As winter drags on, I mark off what I think are full days in my book, feeling for the right place to make the mark in the dark. Few words are spoken between us.

Movement is sparse. We conserve energy.

Sleep takes up most of our hours, sometimes an entire day and night, so we can avoid feeling hungry and stretch our meager supplies.

I begin to fear that this is how it will always be.

The fear of death by the SS above or starvation below.

I no longer have a physical reaction to Leon. When he is near, nothing registers like before. We speak little.

The months are like dark dreams, the kind that carry over into that just-waking state, when you are unsure where you are, who you are, and whether you are awake or asleep.

We run out of candles and become so low on kerosene that we are forced to make rules as to when we are allowed to use light.

We become experts at moving about the caves in total darkness, memorizing cracks and crags and turns, even more so than before.

The children try to find their way to the Land of Israel, but are not allowed to wander too far and are sad when they can't find it.

Cooking is one of the few times when light is allowed.

I take my egg in my front dress pocket to the cooking cave and pull it out, to gaze at Alla's gift again. It is the only thing of beauty in that dark place. It feeds my eyes.

But the egg isn't just a thing of beauty.

It tells me someone up there cares for me and would welcome me back.

Auntie Maya holds on to her rumor. I hold on to Alla's *pysanka*.

1944–

The dirt-bitter taste of potato skins that give brief resistance to the teeth as you bite through them (we no longer peel them, we need every bit of what is edible); the burnt taste of fried centipedes; the creaking of wood pallets as family members turn over; the soft sighs of the weary adults; the half-hearted cries of hungry children; the murmurings of *tefillah* as the men pray; the high-pitched ringing when no sound can be heard—this is what our days and nights are made of.

Even the stories are worn out, repeated so many times they have become ordinary and predictable.

We lose track of days. I now make marks in the margins of *Joan of Arc*, having run out of room on the back covers and endpapers. They are guesses by now. But it feels like an obligation to mark off something. A weary accomplishment.

We walk back and forth in the cave rooms, pacing slowly like weak, caged animals, so we won't lose our ability to walk. Muscles are losing their tightness. Knees are creaking and calves are shaking.

Soon, our limbs begin to bloom roselike splotches, especially on those of the younger children. Teeth become loose, and gums bleed into the white potato flesh. We can't see the blood, just taste its metallic liquid as it mixes with the food and has to be swallowed.

Papa loses two teeth somewhere in the dirt when they fall out. If something falls on the soft ground and you step on it, it is gone forever in the dark.

"I'm losing my teeth, but I still have my family," he says quietly, after the second one falls.

We become more sensitive to the cool humid caves, and push our pallets together for warmth. Our empty bellies swell.

We suck on small stones to pretend we are eating something. They roll around in my mouth, taunting my tongue, not fooling my brain.

I start to not feel "real," like I am made of air.

Sonia's milk has dried up. She nursed Arashel as long as she could, for many weeks, as a way to keep her baby nourished and not be an extra mouth to feed. But bread is running low. Eventually, the adults and Leon and I give our allotments, which amount to the size of a large marble, to the young mother. She refuses when she has stored up a handful, but we have to offer. She chews them to mush, then transfers bits to the baby.

Mama, trying to stretch out our few remaining supplies, boils an extra pair of Uncle Levi's leather boots, and we drink the foul water for whatever animal fat is left in the hide.

We don't find any more centipedes—we've eaten them all up.

Even the animals outside, above us, skittering around in the earth and in the meadow, have more food in their bellies than we do.

Malnutrition is going to do what the Germans could not do to us, break our spirit and take our lives.

Our natural instinct is to save the young first.

Like the cooking smoke that once wended its way up into the ceiling cracks and out the vent, our will to live is finding its way out of us, too. Papa begins to sense this.

We gather at his instructions in Auntie Maya's cave. Papa tells us to sit in a circle, as we are too weak to stand, and lights a thick candle and places it in the center of the circle on the ground. He has been saving the one final candle for a special occasion. This is it.

Papa says a blessing and puts on his *yarmulke* with the rest of the men. He examines his wool *tallis,* wraps himself in it and says a blessing and some verses, then puts it over his shoulders and says his final meditation.

He looks around, looks at each one of us directly, his bloodshot eyes and splotchy face somewhat unfamiliar. His hair completely gray now, lines like muddy trenches running down his dry cheeks. None of us has energy to say anything.

"This is what we have left to last until spring," he says. "Eight potatoes, a handful of grain and dried berries, one stale loaf of bread, one small piece of moldy, hard yellow cheese, each other, and prayer."

He closes his eyes, and we all draw close and pray when he recites a psalm from the Torah. Even the women join in:

"God is our refuge and strength, a very present help in trouble. Therefore will we not fear, though the earth do change, and though the mountains be moved into the heart of the seas; Though the waters thereof roar and foam, though the mountains shake at the swelling there-of. *Selah!*"

And that is when I feel that light again. It takes me by surprise. My mind is humming with the intonations and the feeling that I am going deep into my frail, flawed body. And from within some central point in my empty stomach, a warm glow begins to spread outward from that center to the ends of my limbs.

"There is a river, the streams whereof make glad the city of God, the holiest dwelling-place of the Most High. God is in the midst of her, she shall not be moved; God shall help her, at the approach of morning. Nations were in tumult, kingdoms were moved; He uttered His voice, the earth melted. . . ."

It's hard to describe the feeling, other than as a warmth and an internal image of orange light. It's as if someone else were inside me, someone or something bigger than I am. And it's letting me know again that I am not alone. That no matter what happens, under the earth or on its surface, that I am part of the universe. Tears rain down my dry face.

"He maketh wars to cease unto the end of the earth; He breaketh the bow, and cutteth the spear in sunder; He burneth the chariots in the fire. . . ."

I open my eyes and see tears on my father's face, too. I can tell he is having the same feeling. He nods at me, smiles gently, continues his prayer.

"Ohmain," he finishes. So be it. I believe.

When we get down to the berries and four potatoes, we start sucking on the potato slices raw so we can save them and just get some nutrition. The children, with less fat on them to tide them over, are always sleeping, even while eating. It's not unusual to see a child fall over from the sitting position, a half-chewed berry still in her or his mouth.

I try to be like Joan, who endured prison and torture. "A great soul, with a great purpose, can make a weak body strong and keep it so," Mr. Twain wrote.

Our purpose is to stay alive, but we need food or we won't survive. Someone has to take a chance and leave the caves. We have no more money to barter with, either, just my grandmother's ruby ring that I'd received on my fifteenth birthday. I think I must now be sixteen. My guess is it's around February twenty-second. But I say nothing. We've stopped celebrating all birthdays.

But it's as if Mama knows instinctively that it's my day, or around my day. I catch her looking at the ring one night in the kitchen, when she's washing Arashel's diapers. No soap left, just using hot water, but there is little beyond urine that the baby is leaving in the cloth.

She must have taken the ruby from where it had been hidden in her hem.

"Mama, you have to sell it," I say.

She looks up at me, startled. She hadn't heard me enter the cave.

She has aged, too. Her silky hair is now wiry, with specks of white, and with specks of orange from malnutrition. Her hands are dry and covered in the red rash we are used to by now. I don't get to see her face enough these days. I miss it. Especially the softness of her brown eyes, ringed with so many lashes. Her one beauty, she used to say. Her lashes are now gone, but her eyes are still the same.

She slips the red ruby ring on her speckled, skeletal hand. It's loose and the gem looks like another scurvy spot. She sighs.

"This is all I have left of your bubbe."

"You have her pictures," I plead gently. "And you have me and Leeba. Isn't she in us?"

Mama looks at me, her eyes squinting. It is getting harder to see in the caves, even with low light. Our eyes are failing us, lack of food making them weak. She smiles.

"You are right as always, my little ancient soul," she says, drawing me to her. "It's just a ring, but I resent that I have had to give up everything I own, everything, to stay alive in my own country. This should not be. But this is always the way."

"Maybe we are in the wrong country," I say. "Remember when Uncle Levi was talking of Canada?"

"Yes." She twirls a strand of my long hair around her finger. "Yes, maybe you are right. Maybe we Jews can find peace somewhere on this planet. Maybe some already have. I hope they have."

She lets me go and stirs the boiling pot. The ring is still on her finger.

In my half sleep, as the bodies around me start to stir into wakefulness, I hear a crunching sound and then Symon's cry of "Oh no!"

My heart leaps into my mouth. *My egg is under the pallet safely, isn't it?*

"Hanna?"

"Yes, Symon?" I mutter.

"It's . . . your egg, I think. It feels like I broke it. It must have rolled out from under the bed."

I lie still for a moment, as if movement would make it true.

Then I scootch down to the foot of the pallet and make my way carefully to the side, where he is. I crawl on my knees, feeling ahead of me with one hand till I run into his leg. He takes my hand and guides it to the ground by his foot. There, indeed, are the sharp shards of my beautiful *pysanka*. But there is something else, too. It feels like paper.

I feel around in the soft dirt and gather the paper rounds and flatten them out on my thighs. It feels . . . like money.

"Papa!" I reach for his large body under the quilts on the next pallet over.

We have to light a precious match. It *is* money. I count three *złotych* bank notes, worth 150 *złotych* in total. Alla managed to insert some notes into the egg, and had sealed the hole over with a large plug of wax. I had been surprised to see the wax seal was larger than normal, and still on the egg, but thought nothing of it.

Dear Alla. It must be a good portion of her *pysanka* money. Perhaps this egg would not save the world, but it would get us through the rest of the winter and save Mama from having to sell our last valuable possession.

I would so dreadfully miss this gift that kept me going, but the knowledge she cares so much is better than the dyed messages. It gives all of us an emotional lift. Everyone wants to see the *pysanka* fragments, to hear the story of Symon stepping on them again on his way to relieve himself. Symon goes from being a villain to a hero, and he loves it, puffing out his thin chest.

With my permission, Mama grounds the egg fragments

into powder and puts a bit of it in all our water. She says it will be good for us. I drink the chalky water, thinking of Alla in her warm kitchen, aglow with candles and lanterns. Thinking of the Ziz, who spreads its wings in protection.

How I wish I could see homelight again.

It is the Cohan brothers who have the most strength and muscle left to leave the caves and make the trek to a few nearby farmers who have sold us some of their goods before. And it is the brothers who have better eyesight, which is needed to read facial expressions. "We no longer trust words," they say to us. "We trust faces." They return to peasant farmers who were once sympathetic and have some goodwill left in their eyes.

Some of the local Ukrainians who had turned on us were now seeking to completely eradicate us as the Russians approach. Papa had heard the Ukrainians repeat, as they buried the dead in the forest clearing, "If there is no accuser, there will be no judge." They do not want to face the consequences of a Russian take back. Mama says the irony is that the Russians had once tried to eradicate us themselves, but now they would be our liberators, if they could make the Germans retreat.

The twins return with three candle stubs, and small sacks of oats, cracked corn, and winter wheat. But better than that, they have a few jars of pickled cucumber slices and sweet peppers one peasant farmwife had in her cellar and could spare. We've learned that it is late March, that the long, spirit-crushing winter is nearly over.

We savor those pickled delicacies, suck on the juices, almost swoon on the salty vinegar, bits of aromatic pepper and garlic, and sweetness from the red peppers. And we savor the knowledge that the Russians are indeed moving in.

"*L'chaim!* To life!" We toast with jars of vinegar, for the first time since the invasion, because now we start to really believe life might continue.

"The Russians already swept Kwasova free of Germans last month, but we did not know it. In any case, the Germans came back again. So it's best we did not leave," Pavel explains.

Jacob continues, "You can hear the cannon and machine-gun fire at night and see the sky lighting up in the distance over Kwasova. The Russians have returned. It is something, to see so much orange light and hear so much artillery up on the surface. Nothing penetrates down here."

"The farmers say we are due for a large snowstorm this week, which will make it easier for the Red Army to move in. It is just a matter of time. Even some German soldiers are deserting, trying to hide as villagers. We just need to hold on a little bit longer," Pavel says firmly.

"Have you heard anything about Levi?" Auntie Maya asks.

The twins shake their head no at the same time and in the same direction. It is the one bit of news, or lack of news, that isn't good on that night.

The candles flicker against the rock cavern, making us glow. Our shrunken stomachs are almost full for the first time in months, and again we have hope. Maybe we can go home. Maybe we can live above ground again.

While we wait for possible freedom, our mood lifts slightly. It's hard to keep the human spirit down for long, at least the spirit of those of us who have the instinct to survive. We have heard of many who gave up, some who committed suicide in the woods. We don't judge anyone in these circumstances, but what holds *us* together?

Papa would say it is due to the strength in our culture, the importance we give to our family connections and our faith. How not compromising one's beliefs and values makes strength of its own. "Quiet water can break the river banks," he loves to repeat when we become discouraged.

We sleep less, and start telling stories again.

Tell me a story . . .

Mama: "This is the story of the crane and the fox. I have not told this one to you before, and you will soon see why.

"A crane met a fox in the forest. The crane said, 'Take me in for the winter, little fox, and I'll teach you to fly.'

"The fox took him into his lair.

"But one day, hunters discovered the crane and fox were together in the lair, and they began to dig down into it.

"The fox asked the crane how many ideas he had to escape. The crane said, 'One.'

"'What is it?' asked the fox.

"'I will lie down near the entrance and play dead. They will pick me up and look me over. Just then, you run out of the lair and they will drop me as they take chase to you. Then I'll fly away and you run away.

"The hunters found the dead crane. 'Look,' they cried, 'the fox has killed the crane.'

"Just then, the fox dashed out of the lair and headed for the forest. And the crane flew into the sky."

As Mama tells this story by candlelight, the children gathered in her arms and at her feet, I see her eyes lift to the cavernous ceiling. All eyes lift, mine included. To be free of this lair someday. To be able to dash or fly off somewhere, anywhere.

Have we outwitted the hunters?

We would soon find out.

Papa sticks the *Tzeler* out every night, then looks out when no shots are fired, to try to listen for the progress of the Red Army.

"Still hear cannon fire," he says one night.

Another night he says, "There is soot floating in the air. I see many fires near the town and on the main road."

A few weeks after the Cohan brothers returned, and we begin to run low on food again, Papa decides it's time to sneak out to Yuri's Witness Tree, to see if there is a message. We all hold him close, remembering Uncle Levi. Leon volunteers to follow him with an axe, but Papa shakes his head no.

We wait, nibbling on some stale *varenyky*—dumplings made from flour and water—because we think it is a Saturday and we can't light the cooking fire. Being in the warmish cave, with access to more supplies, we are back to honoring our traditions in any way we can.

Hours go by. Mama breaks tradition of no work on a Sabbath and sews some patches onto Symon's pants and some porcelain buttons back on to some dresses and shirts while we still wear them; Sonia plays with Arashel, who is less splotchy now and crawls on weak, unsteady legs and arms; Mr. Stadnick reads; the Cohan brothers whittle some wood branches they'd collected; Leon draws in the margins of his book; and I watch them all.

I want to remember this, how we were when we lived like the fox. I want this to be the same folktale of survival.

We hear whistling before we see his light. Then Papa is amongst us, lifting the children and crying and hugging Mama and Auntie Maya. We cry, watching him cry. We don't even know why yet. His emotion is so contagious, and we breathe with him. His bottom lip trembles. He sinks to his knees, clutches his hands together, raises his face to the overhanging rock. Papa can't speak for a long time. He takes deep breaths, trying to control his emotions, knowing we are waiting . . . holding ours.

"It's done," he finally gasps out. "The Germans are gone for good. Yuri left the sun and a Russian sickle on the tree. That means Kwasova and all surrounding areas have been taken back by the Red Army. We can go home now. We can go *home* now!"

APRIL 30, 1944—

How do you leave a place of safety, a place that has surrounded you like your mother's dark womb, a place that gave you life in the form of water, and a chance to grow in freedom? We are excited, of course, but also a bit tentative. We've grown so used to shutting out the world and living in darkness. The younger children have forgotten the upper world almost entirely. Little Arashel has never known it.

Four homes were made under the earth, and we can't bring everything with us. Once again, we just have our own bodies and the clothes on our backs, and a few things that we need to survive and that we can carry. Mama takes the house key she'd kept, and her sewing kit. The men take the cooking equipment and tools and lanterns. The women carry the bedding and the few food supplies that are left. The children take their *motanky* dolls, now ragged and grimy with cave dirt. But they won't part with them. I bring my book.

We leave behind the pallets to rot, shoes that have lost a mate, utensils that were lost in the dirt, rags, buckets, and Papa's teeth.

For the first time in more than twelve months, we are all fully awake and ready to leave the lair in the daytime as a family. We follow Papa to the new exit.

Butterflies soar in my stomach. For some reason I think of the moth that sat on my knife blade, the night I did not sleep on the edge of the meadow and waited for death.

Papa climbs the stairway made of piled rocks to remove the board hiding the hole. It scrapes back.

Daylight shines down so powerfully it makes me close my eyes and step back, even though I want nothing more than to move ahead.

When it's my turn to climb to the top, my stomach's butterflies are in fast motion. Leon is at the surface before me. He holds out his hand from the tall grass surrounding the hole.

I barely see him. The light is so bright, it's white. It burns. I stumble, shielding my eyes. He catches my elbow.

"Careful," he says. "You'll get used to it soon."

As I wait by the hole to watch the others crawl out and get

lifted to a standing position, I gradually open my eyes to the sunlight. First the blur goes away. Then, there is grass. Then, trees in the distance. Then, the meadows and the mountains in the distance. I look up to the sky, shielding my eyes. I have to see the blue, even if it hurts.

The children whimper when they are lifted out, hiding their faces in their parents' skirts and pants. Arashel is terrified.

"It hurss," Golda cries, rubbing her eyes. "Put out the lantern!"

Auntie Maya smiles and hugs her. "It is not a lantern, Golda, it is the sun, up in the sky, the opposite of the moon. We can't turn it off. Only God can. Or the clouds."

We all look at each other, smiling. We are a ragged bunch. We haven't seen each other in bright light for so long. Our eyes are so damaged that we didn't realize how much we'd aged, grown pale and thin, and how dirty our clothes are. We look like dusty miners. But we still smile. We are alive.

Some snow patches remain, scattered around in the meadow, and we wash what dirt we can off our faces and hands, using grass to beat the dust and mud from our skirt and pant hems. We're going to be seen by other people now, and we want to look as best as we can.

The road back into Kwasova is littered with smoking military equipment. We walk warily around burned out tanks, trucks, and cannons. It's like walking through an apocalyptic scene, hazy with acrid smoke and the nauseating smell of petrol. It's Pavel who guesses what happened.

"They couldn't retreat with all this heavy equipment in the March snow storm, but they burned it all, so we can't use it against them."

All around us, machines that had carried out so much death. Black smoking sentinels, like the minions that help the serpent in Alla's story of evil.

As we approach town, a new anxiety takes hold. *What will we find?*

No one passes our ragged group on the road. We head to our house. Not wanting to be separated yet, everyone follows us. Mama gasps when we step over the rise near the farm. Alla's whitewashed cottage stands untouched across the street. But our home, Mama's pride and joy, is a shell of what used to be the house and barn.

My feet and my spirit feel suddenly tired and heavy. There will be no home to return to. No bed, not even a roof over our heads. No place to rehang the *mezuzah*. We walk slowly toward the skeleton.

The locals stripped it of its doors, glass windows, bricks, and shingled roof. Even the floorboards are gone, the sink, the iron stove. Even the chimney's fieldstones were removed.

Nothing remains.

Mama stands before the house, the large iron key in her hand. She drops it in the front yard dirt.

Papa looks at the rest of the crowd. "They did not think we were coming back."

Jacob shakes his head. "I didn't see all this in the dark. I'm sorry. There was no moon out that night, and I came from behind Alla's house so as not to be seen. And her shutters were closed."

"Hanna!" I hear a cry behind me.

Alla, in a shuffle-run across the road, into my arms. Her good sweet smell, her large bosom. A dog's bark behind her, and Ovid is jumping all over Symon and licking his face.

Alla puts her hands on either side of my head and looks into my eyes. "I had great hope you would survive," she says. She kisses me on my forehead, standing on her toes to reach me. (I am now taller than she is.) "Great hope."

"I missed you, Alla," is all I can say in return, so happy to be seeing her again that I hug her twice. I pull back then and look into her eyes. "Was it a phoenix, or the Ziz?"

Her eyes crinkle and her smile is wide. "Whatever gave you hope."

After the commotion dies down, she invites us into her small cottage for barley soup. She doesn't have enough bowls to go around, so we share. It is the best soup we have ever had.

"Beats shoe leather, huh?" Leon jokes.

It is the first joke anyone has told in months.

Some have to stand while eating. But this is a bit of home. We do have something to return to, someone who is happy to see us.

We spread out through the *shtetele*. It is hard to split up, like watching parts of yourself go. The Stadnicks still have a roof on their home, because the Germans had been stationed there. But after they retreated, some Ukrainians claimed it. The Stadnicks talk them into allowing them back in to the upper floor in exchange for not contesting the takeover. The Cohans and Polina decide to keep walking over the Polish border, following the Red Army. The Rabinowitzes leave for the next village over, where Sonia was raised, knowing they will not find her family alive.

I say good-bye to Arashel, who has stopped crying and keeps pointing to things with a question in her eyes. She is a smart little girl. Now that she has started turning into a little person, I know why people want to have children. I'm so glad she has a chance to grow up.

Auntie Maya won't leave us. Her house is also occupied. Our sheep sheds are empty and still standing, so she and Mama clean them out and we move our small lot of belongings into the sheds. We have the outhouse still, and while the blue pump had been stolen from the water well, we can still use a tin bucket that Alla gives us to retrieve the water. Once again, we are lucky. The well has not been poisoned, as some wells had been by the SS when they retreated. We were warned to stay away from the ones in the market square.

Not much is left of the valuables that Symon buried in the sheds' corners. Most valuables had already been dug up and sold, but Papa digs around just in case, and finds a set of my bubbe's silver spoons.

The sheds are better than the caves, though my young cousins have trouble adjusting to sleeping at night and being awake during a sunny day. But over a few weeks' time, they get used to the new routine and begin to explore the area, running far and wide, climbing trees, relearning how to be young and free.

I am jealous of how quickly they forget.

Life does not magically rework itself, however. We can't get our horse back. Steed was butchered to feed the miller's family through the hard winter.

As we venture into town, neighbors stare, as if we're ghosts. And I suppose we are. They thought we were dead. We aren't supposed to be alive. Many of our Ukrainian and Polish neighbors turn from us in shame. The wood synagogue has been destroyed.

Mama sees her favorite dress on Mrs. Davydenko one market day. They both turn away from each other.

Everything now feels rearranged, out of place.

Rumors of Ukrainian bands of assassins trickle into town. Roaming the countryside, they are attacking and killing the few remaining Jews as they make their way out of hiding. In our valley the Russian soldiers try to stop them, but the assassins are still able to find some who are unprotected.

When I'm in town getting bread, I see a few survivors walk in from meadow and forest bunkers, bent over because they've been in such cramped spaces for so long. It is heartbreaking to see these crippled survivors, who can no longer stand straight, shuffle into town with nothing but the rags on their backs.

We do what we can for a few of them, and the healthier ones most often move on to another town or village, but the weaker ones stay as beggars, crooked and hunched over, lying in the street gutters. The whites of their eyes are always there, showing. Because of what those eyes have seen, these survivors' expressions are frozen in permanent fear.

Some Polish and Ukrainian men that the Russians sent away, fearing they would rebel, come back from Siberian gulags with tattoos all over their necks and faces. Bold marks that call out to those who see them that there was one way in which they could control their bodies.

Fascinated, I stare at the dark lines and words, inked art that tells their own stories.

I'm no longer innocent. I now know why some Kwasovians had been disappearing on the trains.

The news of the marauding bands leaves everyone uneasy. Some neighbors choose to sleep in the orchards at night rather than in their beds to avoid being murdered in their sleep.

We did not survive the war to be killed by our own countrymen.

Fear is still with us, even a year later, but we celebrate with the world when Germany surrenders on May 7, 1945.

Papa gathers our family under the orchard trees, heavy with summer fruit. "This is not our home any longer," he says sadly. "It is time to leave Ukraine."

Mama sighs. "I knew this was coming."

"Where will we go?" Auntie Maya asks.

"The Russians are allowing Jews and Ukrainian Poles to resettle in Poland, so we should prepare to leave once again for a DP, a displaced persons camp. From there, I can arrange passage for us to New York City, in America. We will make the overseas journey in two groups, as they will not let us out all at once. First Eva, with Leeba and Symon and Olena. Then I will go with Maya, Hanna, Golda, and Little Natan."

We shift around on the grass, uncomfortable at the thought of being separated for the first time in three years. I dig my hands into the dirt and look up at the green apples forming like globes above us. I thought this place could be ours again. I thought we could get back what we owned, what was rightfully ours.

"And there is one more thing I need to say." He clears his throat. We know this means he is not going to say something good. "We are going to change our names."

"What?" we all cry together.

"It is time for this, also. The Talmud says that there are four things that can change your fate. They include changing your deeds, and changing your name. Abram changed his name to Abraham. We should change our names to change our fate. It is still not safe to be Jewish, and it will be easier to obtain a visa to leave the country if we take on different names."

And with that decision, I become Marcelina Borowski, a young woman with a Polish birth certificate and passport, made by an expert forger from Warsaw for the fee of one silver spoon.

Father returns to Alla her land and all the buildings on it as a thank you for helping save our lives more than once.

"I don't want this," she says to him, when he hands her the signed note. "But I will accept it for your peace of mind."

"You must," he insists, "for I cannot repay you any other way. Except to say I believe you may be a *tzaddik*, one of the righteous among us. You saved many lives at great cost to yourself. You will always be in our prayers."

Before we leave for the DP camp in July, I prepare myself to say good-bye to my best friend, Leon. His family has decided to stay in Ukraine, though they plan to move to a new village and change their names as well.

We walk down to the old empty schoolyard, and sit under our tree. School will start up again in the fall, and Comrade Stalin's poster will be repasted on the walls. But so much has changed.

We have changed.

Looking at that desolate, dusty schoolyard from our past is like looking at the ghosts of our former selves.

We say nothing for a long time. Till unwanted tears start to rain into my clenched hands.

"Hanna," he sighs, wrapping his thin arms around me. "You did it. You helped keep us safe. Thank you for being my friend. Thank you for being you. Look at me."

I try to look, but he's just a watery blur.

"We will always be friends. How can we not be? No one knows what we went through. I will *always* be there for you."

"How? You will be across the ocean. And I am not Hanna anymore—I'm Marcelina."

He laughs. "And I am Mykola. Mykola will write to Marcelina. We will have good lives and be happy for each other. Our names have changed our fate, remember?"

I nod.

"And you will always be the first woman I kissed."

Together, holding hands, we leave the schoolyard behind us forever.

Auntie Maya made us wait as long as possible before going to the DP camp so she could get final word of Uncle Levi. Papa checked in neighboring towns and used his new contacts in Poland to see if he could find any word of him, but returned with no news. It was time to move on.

We will never know what became of him. It is a burden I will carry for the rest of my life. I have nightmares. I wake, sweating and shaking. It is he who haunts me. And smoke plumes rising from chimneys. And rapid-fire gunshots. And dark serpents. Why was *he* taken, and not me? I wonder. Am I allowed to be happy, even though he is gone?

When I visit a new town or city, I always look for him in windows and scan the faces of passersby. Even after I have forgotten his face, I still look for it, hoping I will recognize him in some way. I say his name aloud, quietly and privately, every Friday when the sun goes down. "Levi Yurkovich."

When someone gives up his or her life for you, they are always part of you.

On the day my family left Ukraine, I held Alla Petrovich in my arms one last time, felt her warmth, breathed in deeply to remember the smell of beeswax and candle soot that always surrounded her, held her rainbow hands. My dear Alla, who is my real talisman. Whose center is pure and full of light. I received letters from her after we arrived in New York. Each one mentioned the colors of the steppe, which she said were returning after years of Nazi pillage and burning. And she included in all of them a carefully written inventory of the *pysanky* she had made.

"I am making many this year, so we will all be safe."

Before the letters stopped, she gave me another *pysanka*, to replace the broken one. *Pysanky,* or *pysaty*, means "to write." This was Alla's most important message to me. An especially large goose egg, it sits under a small glass dome in our living room, on a bed of maroon velvet.

You love to ask me about it, daughter. I twirl it around and tell you about the signs. About the explosion of red poppies, which mean joy and beauty, and the blue diamonds that circle the top and bottom, meaning knowledge. And about how nature can be your friend and help you survive. How faith and family should be your greatest weapon against the world. There will always be serpents.

Your father—my husband. Alla's wax prophecy came true. I was rocked back and forth in the steamship we took from Poland in 1945, until I caught scarlet fever. When we arrived on Ellis Island, the ruby ring sewn into the hem of my long skirt, I was pulled aside during health inspection, flushed and feverish, and sent to the island hospital to be quarantined. A doctor, a white coat, a gentle, cool hand. Two years later, at nineteen, I wore the ruby ring as a promise of our engagement, then married the kind doctor and became Marcelina Rosenberg.

Your grandparents, who are the main reason I am alive, are gone, but they lived to see grandchildren born, their greatest joy and their best revenge, they said, to see life continue. My Auntie Maya remarried and moved her family to Canada, which I think Uncle Levi would have approved of. But as you know, your aunt Leeba and uncle Symon remain close by. My little sister, the seamstress and mother of her own children, and my protective little brother, the police officer who makes sure others are safe now.

My friend Leon kept his promise to me, sending papery-thin airmail notes with little sketches. Automobiles, garden flowers, birds, small chubby portraits of his very well-fed children.

Only 5 percent of our people survived the Holocaust in all of Ukraine, and only 2 percent in Galicia, in Western Ukraine. We Slivkas are, however, among the few who survived as a complete family. I like to think we survived because the earth cared for us and protected us from much of the horrors above its surface. I like to think we survived because we stayed together at all costs, and kept each other going. We were also just plain lucky to have stayed one step ahead of our pursuers. I wish all of us had been so lucky.

We also cannot forget the help of those few special neighbors who risked their own lives to feed us and save us. I wish all the Yuris and Allas of the world would multiply like her eggs, break open and spread forth.

Good people need each other.

The Story Ends

TELL ME A STORY...
My name is Hanna Slivka. I was born on February twenty-second, in the winter of 1928.

I am still breathing.

This is my story.

A Historical Note

All the characters in this book are fictional, but for Adolf Hitler and the Gestapo chief, Koelner. However, the story was inspired by the powerful matriarch Esther Stermer and her extended family, and four other families (aged two to seventy-six), who survived World War II and the invasion of the Wehrmacht by hiding in bunkers and, later, in two underground caves. Their story is captured in the award-winning documentary *No Place on Earth*, which outlines the discovery of their history by American caver Christos Nicola, and includes interviews with survivors.

After I viewed the film, their family story of survival and transcendence would not let me go. I wanted to bring it out in the form of a novel for young readers and adults. But when I began writing five years ago, life was relatively peaceful, with a respected person of color as US president. Little did I know that my agent and I would be submitting the final manuscript during a time in which the KKK and White Nationalists would march again and bring forth from the depths of an ugly, deadly history their rallying racist and anti-Semitic chants and their anti-Semitic acts, some violent, by an increase of 57 percent in 2017. I dream of a day when we will no longer need Holocaust stories to remind us to be kind to each other, and to be watchful of those who aren't.

My *shtetele* (or small town) is fictional, but "Kwasova" was the name of an actual Ukrainian village or town, long gone now. It remains only on very old maps. I also wanted to send my fictional family into the forest to which many Jews fled. The Stermers did not do this, which was a good thing as many of the Jews who hid in forests were eventually hunted down by the SS or Ukrainian rogue bands, or they died of malnourishment and the skin diseases that plagued the character Polina. Instead, the Stermers fled first to one cave, which they abandoned for safety reasons, then to another. The second cave was a better living situation as it had good ventilation and did indeed have underground lakes, hence their name for it: The Grotto, or Priest's Grotto (the cave was on the land of a retired priest).

This "Gypsum Giant," or grotto cave (in actuality a series of cave rooms seventy-seven miles long, one of the longest in the world), is the setting for the third part of my novel, and many of the survival skills and details of their life underground come firsthand from the Stermers. The women and children of the grotto hold the record of 511 days of underground living in both caves (my story has the family live underground in this Grotto for about thirteen months, almost 400 days), or 344 days of continuous living in the grotto alone. Few expert cavers have lasted more than a couple of months in similar conditions. Many who tried have experienced the same psychological trauma that prisoners who are put in isolation experience.

There is one other character based on a real man. Yuri Jańowski is based on a friendly forester named Munko who helped the Stermers by revealing the cave locations as hiding spots and by keeping their secret while being their contact to the outside world. There were in fact many foresters in the

District of Galicia who helped to hide Jews, although records of survivors are few. Munko was also the one who told the Stermers it was safe to leave their cave, when the Germans left for good, by dropping a bottle down the entrance with a note in it. I chose instead to use Yuri's Witness Tree, whose history I came across doing research for another story. Signs, or messages, on trees are scientifically termed *arborglyphs*; they are a rather recent discovery and it's unclear how many centuries these "Witness Trees" (aspen, silver birch, Scots pine, lodgepole pine, and beech) have been used to communicate messages, but research is underway and there is proof that Native Americans and sheepherders across the continents have used this method of messaging for centuries. While Jewish law prohibits creating "graven images," the tradition of carving religious words onto trees does appear in several legends of Polish-Jewish history, as retold by Uncle Levi. I discovered this legend of origin late in the process of writing this book, in Haya Bar-Itzhak's *Jewish Poland*, and it gave the tree carvings more symbolic meaning.

The Stermers lost touch with Munko after the war, and I like to think he disappeared into his own forest.

Another piece of history that has gone relatively unnoticed is the existence of Counters: *Zähler* (German), or *Tzeler* (Yiddish, derived from *tseylm*, "to count"). I chose to use *Tzeler*, as quoted in Father Patrick Desbois's groundbreaking book *The Holocaust by Bullets*. Counters were commissioned or forced by the Germans to count and record Jews for roundups and the bodies of the dead. Counters were both Jews and non-Jews, and were often killed, according to Desbois, so there would be no one to report the massive numbers of victims. Perhaps this is one reason so little is known about them. I hope my lamplighter's story serves to literally shine some light on the gruesome role of the lost and forgotten *Tzelers*.

The ancient art of decorating eggs, *pysanky* (sometimes appearing plural as *pysankas*), is found in many Eastern European cultures. All the decorating methods described in this book are based on old Ukrainian tools and dyes, and the folklore and *pysanky* symbolism I incorporate hail from the Carpathian region.

I have done my best to be historically accurate in as many ways as possible, and just about everything that happens in this book happened to either the Stermers or to other Jews. But I was challenged by the lack of research on the small villages and towns of Ukraine. There were few survivors to pass along accounts of the events that took place in the outer reaches of the steppe lands, and few kept records, because paper was scarce and precious and only wealthy city or ghetto dwellers could pay for it on the black market or have access to the scraps that were often used to record their history, thoughts, or Nazi atrocities. Compound that with the fact that Ukraine and Russia kept much of this information hidden until about two decades ago. Also, many of the oral accounts in English don't include the specific, everyday details that I needed. Therefore I relied heavily on the Stermer memoir and verified as much as I could with survivors and their families, and with historians.

To those who like to ferret out historical inaccuracies, I say this: Remember this is fiction, and in order to tell a "story," sometimes one has to slightly bend timelines or small historical details, and as the audience is mainly young adults, I left out some of the more nightmarish events. What I did learn was that each village and town had its own traditions, its own mix of cultures that was successful to differing degrees, and its own experience during the Holocaust. I consider the Stermers lucky to have come from a town where Jews were more integrated into the community than in other towns, and to have been in an area geographically that appears to have avoided the C and D killing groups of the Einsatzgrüppen advance in 1941, which bought them more time to hide and escape. However, even their town may have been subject in July 1941 to an initial raid from the German army, which began their persecution. I left this potential raid out, in keeping with the history of some of the smaller towns that did not get the full force of the Waffen-SS or Gestapo until later. Note that I say "may have." Another thing I learned in this process is that memory can be both elusive and photographic. There are different variations on dates and events so it's hard to pin down with 100 percent accuracy all the historical events that took place. We can only gather the common threads together until more research is complete.

It was a great honor for me to tell this story, and to be able to come into contact with some of the most remarkable people I have ever met.

Finally, while Alla Petrovich is fictional, she became one of my favorite characters in the book, perhaps because, for me, she symbolizes all that is good in this world. It's estimated that only 5 percent of Ukrainian Jews, and only 2 percent of Western Ukrainian Jews, survived, with almost no families intact. This makes the survival of the whole Stermer family even more remarkable (though, tragically, Esther's husband was killed by local Ukrainians after their triumphant return above ground). And if there were survivors such as the Stermers (some are still alive today), it was often because there was an Alla or a Yuri in the background either offering small gestures of food and clothing or actively helping their fellow human beings hide or escape. Many Ukrainians, Poles, and peasants—both adults and children and entire townships or villages—were brutally shot, burned, or hung from trees and street signs and lampposts. It was punishment for harboring or assisting Jews and meant to serve as a warning to others who might wish to help. It should also be noted that records exist of Ukrainian police who defied German orders and saved Jews.

As Hanna says, may more of the Allas and Yuris multiply to keep the serpent at bay.

And as the grandchildren of Esther Stermer write at the end of her memoir (*We Fight to Survive*) about keeping her family alive and together:

Yasher koach, Bubbie Esther! (Good Job!)

Acknowledgments

It can take a village to raise a child, and the same can be said for a book. My thanks to the following villagers: Memorial Hall Library in Andover, Massachusetts, for helping me procure the rare copy of Esther Stermer's memoir from the Library of Congress. Without it, I would not have been able to write with as much authenticity as I was able to manage. Journalist Paul Goldberg (author of *The Yid*) spent much time obsessing with me via email over the right epithet to use against Hanna in the opening scene. I appreciate his humor and expertise in language. Helen Winkler discussed Yiddish dances with me and pointed me toward Andriy Nahachewsky, Huculak Chair of Ukrainian Culture and Ethnography at the Kule Folklore Centre at the University of Alberta, Canada. Andriy was kind enough to spend many hours explaining Jewish dance and general culture in Ukraine. I appreciate what the Kule center does to preserve history. The Holocaust Memorial Resource and Education Center of Florida is a sobering museum to visit. But their resources are exceptional, and the staff generous with their time. Special thanks to Mitchell Bloomer and Pam Kancher. Magda Mizgalska at the POLIN Museum of the History of Polish Jews also wrote back with helpful information. Jewish Records Indexing–Poland provided important information on the school system in the Stermer town, and Megan Lewis, reference librarian for the US Holocaust Memorial Museum, assisted with vital research material..

My wonderful book blurbers were invaluable in more ways than one. Not only were they willing to blurb, despite busy schedules, but their words kept me going when I needed support. Thank you, Crystal Chan, Bobbie Ann Mason, Sharon Hart-Green, Elizabeth Wein, and Greg Dawson. Special thanks to Helen Maryles Shankman, Diney Costeloe, and Tilar Mazzeo not just for blurbing, but also for providing historical advice. Amaryah Orenstein did a helpful edit for historical accuracy and Yiddish terms. Michelle Elvy and Bernard Heise added their expertise in Holocaust and military history. Writer John Guzlowski offered information on Polish foresters, Mary Gannett gave marketing advice, and Sheree Roth, a distant relative of the Stermers, shared her family history and assisted with information as well.

M. J. Rose is a generous mentor; I appreciate her friendship and early assistance. And Beth Hoffman, such a beautiful spirit, also was generous with advice. Marsha Skrypuch corrected a *pysanky* error and increased my knowledge of collaborators. My mother, Sandra Masih, kept championing the book as I wrote, and while my father did not live to see it accepted, his early belief in my imagination and creativity gave me the confidence necessary to tackle such an immense topic. Sister friends Mary Slechta and Tara Laskowski traveled with me through the ups and downs of this project, as did my wonderful agent, Kerry D'Agostino of Curtis Brown, Ltd. I can't thank Kerry enough (and her colleagues at CBL) for believing in and championing this manuscript. I also owe a huge amount of gratitude to Mandel Vilar Press, especially publisher Robert Mandel and senior editor Dena Mandel, who saw the historical importance of this story and brilliantly shepherded it to its present polished form, with the help of their talented staff, Sophie Appel (who created a luminous cover and stunning interior design under the creative direction of Barbara Werden), copyeditor Mary Beth Hinton, and publisher's assistant Lauren Sweeney.

I thank my husband, Michael Gilligan, who is my anchor in life, and my son, Arun Padykula, who is my joy.

But my greatest thanks go to two families, the Dichters and the Dawsons. The Dichter family welcomed me with open arms and tea served in a Polish tea cup. They gave me their time and their stories and their trust, which I don't take lightly. I did not live through the Holocaust, but Wilhelm Dichter (award-winning author of *God's Horse and the Atheists' School*) allowed me into a private place and shared some important feelings that I hope will translate to the page. He also patiently redirected me historically as I had gone off track at the beginning of the book (geography was always my worst subject in school!). I thank his wife, Ola, for her warmth and her own stories, and their son Julius for his enthusiasm and help as well. And to the Dawsons, Greg and Candy: not only did Greg blurb my book while on a writing deadline, but he and his wife allowed me to "borrow" some details from his own book (*Hiding in the Spotlight*) about his mother's life. Zhanna Arshanskaya, herself a Holocaust survivor, was an amazing woman. She treasured her copy of *Joan of Arc*, and survived by being pushed from a death march by her father (Polina's story). Both Wilhelm's and Greg's books (cited in the Reader's Guide, which is free and available to download from the press's homepage) are highly recommended. I am not the same person after reading them.